SOUTH OF ELFRIDA

South of Elfrida

HOLLEY RUBINSKY

BRINDLE
& GLASS

Brindle & Glass Publishing Ltd.
brindleandglass.com

LIBRARY AND ARCHIVES CANADA CATALOGUING IN PUBLICATION
Rubinsky, Holley, 1943–
South of Elfrida / Holley Rubinsky.

Short stories.
Also issued in electronic format.
ISBN 978-1-927366-05-9

I. Title.

PS8585.U265S69 2013   C813'.54   C2012-906799-7

Editor: Rhonda Batchelor
Proofreader: Heather Sangster, Strong Finish
Design: Pete Kohut
Cover image: Arin Ringwald

Brindle & Glass is pleased to acknowledge the financial support for its publishing
program from the Government of Canada through the Canada Book Fund, Canada
Council for the Arts, and the Province of British Columbia through the British
Columbia Arts Council and the Book Publishing Tax Credit.

MIX
Paper from
responsible sources
FSC
www.fsc.org   FSC® C016245

The interior pages of this book have been printed on 30% post-consumer
recycled paper, processed chlorine free, and printed with vegetable-based inks.

1 2 3 4 5 17 16 15 14 13

PRINTED IN CANADA

Yuri

CONTENTS

The Arribada

The ragged fronds from palms along the strand twist in the breeze as Leonard walks his nine-year-old niece down the beach to the fenced turtle enclosure, his toes and hers sticky with sand. The turtle enclosure is made of finely meshed wire so the turtles can't escape when they hatch. The gate is kept locked and wire is attached to the top to prevent the theft of eggs, a local delicacy. In the sand, beside the mounds, there are ice cream sticks with labels, noting dates, the type of turtle, relative age, and size.

"How do you suppose the eggs get inside the fence?" The child is slight for her age, so the reflective phrasing of her question seems incongruous coming from her lips.

"After the mother turtles lay them, it is the turtle man who collects the eggs from the beach to keep them safe."

"Safe from what?"

"Predators," Leonard says. Her eyes are a remarkable green. She has long, dark lashes and light brown, curly hair. The bruises on her cheeks and upper arms are fading. "There are many kinds of predators—birds as well as people—who hurt the young." She throws him an irritated look before turning away. "The Olive Ridley nests in an arribada," he resumes, using the Spanish word for a group of nests. "The arribadas are a mystery. The egg-bearing females seem to know where to come. It's as though they get a message and then pile up together on this beach where they were born."

"How do they know where to find the beach?"

"Finding. Ah. The greatest mystery. Perhaps the whiff of a familiar wind from offshore tells them."

She runs her palm along the wire enclosure and cocks her chin. "I knew it was you in my room."

She's lying. At the back of her eyes he sees a pool of confusion. He visited his sister when the child was two years old, too young to remember him. Because of the nature of his work, he was able to keep tabs on her. The word *uncle* means nothing to her. She has had too many uncles.

The moment of alarm in her room was followed quickly by willingness. He despairs of the willingness of little girls.

You don't have to be in law enforcement to understand the vulnerability of girls.

He'd left the village with Bianca in the Skylark, an old car in better shape under the hood than it looked from the outside; Leonard had seen to that. The Skylark belonged to the village taxi driver. Bianca, who had children of her own, knew that a little girl could need rescuing. She made arrangements with a nurse at the health clinic to take care of her children for two or three days, depending. Leonard didn't tell Bianca his niece's name because he didn't want her to be implicated, should there be questions in the future. He paid the tolls along the road north, waited patiently in lines while inspectors inspected. They slept in the car on the long ferry ride.

He dropped Bianca off at the Walmart in Nogales, Arizona, and continued on to his sister's shoddy house in south Tucson, notorious at that time for gangs and drugs. He entered the child's bedroom through the window—he had some experience along those lines—and waited for her. The look on her face when she came into the room for her Barbie doll's silver shoes was one of haughty surprise, an expression charming on a little girl.

As they drove back to Nogales, she asked if he had a gold tooth because robbers always had a gold tooth in the stories she wrote for school. She was smug with excitement. He told her he wasn't a robber.

At the prearranged time, he met Bianca outside the Walmart,

surrounded by bags and bags of nonperishable groceries, clothing and toys for her children. They loaded her purchases in the trunk and went into the store together, with the child (named Chastity by her mother; a name he would never call her), to let her choose a brand-new Barbie. Bianca picked a fairy doll and pretended to listen to it. "This dolly tells me she like you very much. She like to go on a trip with you." The child shook her head and chose instead a Barbie Stardoll, a fallen angel, a rebel—strutting in patterned black nylons, wide red streaks in her raven-black hair, wearing a very short, red sateen dress. Bianca put the fairy doll back on the shelf. "Que escandalo!" she sighed. The child peered quizzically at Leonard. "She says you are outrageous, scandalous." His comment made her laugh with wicked delight. Bianca led her into the restroom—by then they were giggling—and changed her into a ruffly pink nylon dress with white lace on the collar. As Leonard had instructed, Bianca stuffed the shorts and T-shirt the child had been wearing into her large handbag. In the car they ate candy corn while Leonard applied light brown makeup to the backs of the child's hands and on her face, his fingers patting gently over the bruise still fresh on her cheek from that scumbag. He combed her brown hair with oil.

The camper where he lives year-round is set under a palm, near enough to the village, yet close enough to hear the ocean all night. The odour of the sea is that of slightly sweet greenness, humid wetness, the flavour of oyster on the tip of the tongue. On their way back she walks ahead. Her small footprints darken the sand.

"Who takes care of them?" She turns and looks back at the egg mounds.

"The turtle man."

She has gradually adapted to limitations—one doll, sketchy TV reception, milk that comes from a can.

"I don't know who you are," she occasionally murmurs.

"I am your real uncle." The old news causes her to shrug. Off and on they have this talk, at the morning market, when they visit Bianca and the children, or at the panaderia, where he allows her to buy sweet, sticky buns.

In the mornings he slides open the six windows, including the two in her sleeping area over the cab of the truck. Her breath is fresh and delicate; her lips rosy. He hesitates. She is so beautiful, so fine. And a new feeling stirs in him: he loves her.

They take their chairs to the sand and put their feet on concrete extrusions from an abandoned building project. She sets her chair far enough from him to indicate she doesn't trust being touched yet; she flinches involuntarily if his hand grazes hers as he passes her a corn tortilla he takes from the iron skillet. Her involuntary movement tells him more than she can. Sometimes when they sit out, watching the ocean, they turn the transistor radio on and listen. One day Leonard introduces the idea of a new name for her. "Chastity is a stupid name," she says. "I don't want a name."

"Every human needs a name."

"Not this Chiquita banana," she says. She sips her can of iced tea; it's tepid due to problems with a propane line to the fridge. He's taken off the panel that accesses the back of the refrigerator and messed with it, then tucked a torn sheet around the exposed fins and wires to keep out the cockroaches.

"Isabella was a queen of Spain. Bella means beautiful."

"I am not beautiful. I don't plan to be beautiful ever. Nothing but trouble."

A hip-hop song comes on the radio: "I wanna do you, girl." "I know that song!" she yelps. Then she sings bars of it, slurring. He thinks she shouldn't know how to sound so sexual. She sings, "'The things I wanna do to you, girl.'" Her shoulders slump, then she throws her head back—like a spasm, a fit— and slip, slide. "'You can do what you like to me,'" she says, "because I'm already dead." She flops onto her side in the sand.

On another day she says, "My bruises are gone," and looks sideways at him, her eyes appraising his. They've taken the aluminum chairs to the water. Surf rolls over their feet. She lifts her T-shirt, looks at her belly and bare chest with its buds of breasts. "Meth whore," she says.

He raises his finger in caution. "No, no. Por favor, don't say that. Forget those words. You're here now." He draws an inverted V in the sand, a simple tent shape. Pokes a little indentation inside. "Lambda," he says. "You are safe here."

She puckers her lips. "Maybe. I like lambs."

He has to laugh. He hopes the wretched events of the past year in particular—his sister, on drugs again, hooked up with another lowlife—will slip away like a tide and leave the surface of the child's mind smooth as fine, wet sand; that happiness is what he wants for her. He wants her to be delighted someday by the memories of her childhood.

He says, "When the eggs hatch, the turtle man won't let the hatchlings crawl to the sea right away. Why would that be?"

"Predators," she says. "Those gulls. Gulls like to eat babies."

The sun falls, a flattened globe, pale orange against a glistening line on the horizon. They drag their chairs back to the camper, leaving tracks in the sand like the Olive Ridley turtles. He takes a beer out of the cooler. The ice has nearly melted. He sighs, puts his feet up on the cooler next to hers. He loves the size of her limbs, her feet with the splayed toes. The odd toes make her unsteady when she runs. Lambda likes her feet bare. Bianca has painted her toenails a little-girl pink.

Sometimes by the fire he talks about his sister and the rebellious girl she was and how it turned out. He speaks in a low tone, falls into his sister's grammar, syntax, her slipshod use of words: "Your mommy did, hey, outrageous things. Hair-raisin' things, wouldn't you say?"

"Yep." Lambda lifts her shoulders and lets them down with a loud sigh that imitates his.

"Did you understand?"

She taps her chin. "Nope."

"You laughed anyway."

"Yep."

He remembers his sister as sometimes being animated and lively. He himself had no idea what the joke was. It doesn't matter now.

Lambda says, "But who are you?" and tilts her chin inquisitively.

She's snoring, whispery little-girl snores. The refrigerator, rattling, works again, though now it has frozen their two eggs in the blue bowl. She wakes as he's looking at the eggs. She comes down the ladder in the pink nylon dress; she's attached to it. It will be small for her soon. She allows him to flick sleepies from the corners of her eyes. "Want some milk?"

"Let's go see the turtles first."

He smiles. She will grow into a woman with priorities.

They reach the wire fence.

"Look," she says, pointing. "One's hatching."

He sees a beak working out of a crack in an egg.

"Look! Two, three. Oh, look, look!"

He says, "Let's go tell the turtle man."

"Let's! Let's go tell the turtle man!" He hears the thrill in her voice. "The turtle man has the key. He'll unlock the gate. He'll save them!"

She runs up the weedy bank to the road and stops the village taxi. "Do you know where the turtle man is, señor?"

The man in the Skylark says, "No, señorita, this hombre, he is a mystery to me."

"Oh, this is not good news for the turtles," Lambda says, her hand on her chin, a parody of a child perplexed.

She looks both ways, crosses the road, and runs up the stairs to Bianca's apartment. Bianca is making coffee in her percolator. "Ah, that mystery man. There is a camper on the beach. Do you know it? He might be there."

They arrive back at the camper. He brushes two fingers across her eyelids. She obediently closes her eyes. He quietly opens the door and steps inside. Lambda, still outside, scratches the screen: "Sir, I am looking for the turtle man."

"Ah, the mystery is solved. Fair señorita, I am he."

"I know," she says. "I knew."

After the sun sets, they take flashlights to the arribada. The dozen hatchlings are clustered in a heap against the mesh. Leonard unlocks the gate and steps inside, carrying a cardboard box. "Hatchlings are appetizers for the sharp-toothed grazers beyond the surf line, but I can't do anything about that," he says. He picks the turtles up, places them in the box, relocks the gate.

Outside the fence, he releases them. They lift their heads and, searching, align themselves slowly toward the ocean. They creep and scratch over the sand until they come to where the land meets the sea. He and Lambda walk behind at a distance. "They have to do this part on their own," he tells her. "It makes them strong, and they learn the scent of home."

In the surf, the tiny turtles tumble. Some return on their backs in the smooth glide of a wave onto the beach. She reaches her hand to turn a baby upright. He shakes his head. "No, my dear. They have to figure it out themselves." Only one or two of the batch will survive, will have the strength to push past the waves and swim the five days and five nights to go beyond the reach of predators. He's ready to tell her all this, his voice grave, when she lets out a shout.

"This one can do it!" Lambda shrieks, pointing to the one he considers the weakest, a hatchling who struggled, upside down, too long. It has flipped on its own and turns a second time, with good speed, toward the sea.

Lambda claps her hands. She looks up at Leonard, delighted. It's so dark, just a few lights from farther up the beach, the stars pressing through the haze, that her face transforms as he stares at her. He sees figures from another time lurking behind her young features, a rose-cheeked barmaid, a princess wearing a robe and crown, and he sees a fair boy grey-faced in the gloaming. Then he fixes on this particular body of this particular child, who is grinning at him as though she knows something, as though she knows what he's about to say. A survivor of this batch will live one hundred years and return to this beach because here she was born and here she was saved.

Among the Emus

Crystal and Colin are into hill country and climbing. They're in Colin's pickup; a little bashed here and there, like they themselves are, is how Crystal thinks of it. She's given a few years to Colin. Before she found him, a man raked thin from hard living and hard work, she'd lost a lot of years to booze. When she pulled herself out of it, she was no longer homely Doreen, acne pits ruining her face, but she was, as she jokes, hanging on to the shirttail of youth.

They're driving up into the north Okanagan to help Angus, Colin's stepson, sell emu oil at the fair. Colin likes to say he mostly raised the boy himself. For the entire drive—all five hours of it so far—Colin has been going on about the Angus-Pure Ranch, its size, what hard work it is for one man because of the animals—emus, bison, yaks, and goats. "Angus says emus are short-sighted. They pick lint off your shirt. I bet you won't go into their pen," Colin tells her.

Crystal doesn't know what an emu looks like. She wonders why anyone would want to go into their pen, anyway. She says, "I wouldn't be afraid." She keeps her eyes on the road.

Colin smacks his hand on the steering wheel. "Jeez, sugar. You get sick from everything and you're scared of everything. You won't go into that pen."

"I'm going in with them, you'll see."

"Look at that pretty little skirt you're wearing. You looking for somebody new at the fair?"

"Yah, so you think," she says and then shuts up. She listens to her earrings tinkle as she shakes her head. Her heart is starting to tremble and quiver.

He says, "Sometimes I wonder if you're too good for me."

A man talking like this is bad. She looks at her feet, in new strappy sandals. She's wearing them so Colin will feel proud when he introduces her to Angus, but no sense explaining such a thing to him. She sips from her bottle of negative-ion water.

She's recently moved from a rented room into Colin's double-wide trailer. His closets are full of clothes from the days he played in a country band—plaid shirts in soft colours with snaps. He has two golden retrievers that he never brushes. He'd never change the sheets if she weren't there to do the wash. She likes doing it, thought he appreciated it, thought they were in love.

Her heart does its flippity-flops and lumpity-lumps like it's trying to get out. Colin says her ailments are all in her mind. Can a person have hyperthyroidism and hypothyroidism at the same time? Crystal—a name she gave herself—has symptoms of both. She's been diagnosed with hypo and prescribed Synthroid. Yet online she reads that two symptoms of hyperthyroidism are anxiety and brittle hair. She has those symptoms too, but it's her heart that worries her the most.

Colin is worthless when she feels sick; he'd as soon open a can of pork and beans for dinner, which leads her to think that all the effort she puts into slow-cooking meat and vegetables is a waste of time. He says he likes her stews. Like? Is that all he can say? His Adam's apple shinnies up and down whenever he starts sweet-talking: "Sugar, I love your stew, bring your little stew over here." And she does.

The country they're driving into is wide-open ranch country, trees in clumps around tidy houses, and a big sky. "It's so pretty," she says. Black Angus cattle graze on the hills. A barking dog runs after the car. Skunkweed fills the ditches alongside the road.

They pass the fairgrounds. Colin says he wants to drop their things off, take a look at the ranch. They swerve off the highway onto an unpaved road and climb. The tires throw stones. A carved wood sign leaning against the fence reads ANGUS-PURE RANCH. They pass the gate, gaping open, and pull into a dirt area between some animal pens and a ranch-style house. The shiny metal roof of the house sparkles, hit by the sun just right. Then dust catches up with them, settles like a swarm of gnats. Colin says, "Look. Emus. Over there." Crystal leans across him. She sees ostrich-like things with waving necks. Colin lets the truck idle. Over the noise of the engine, he clears his throat. "This here is nice country. Angus has got himself good land. A man could like it out here."

She catches the quick look he gives her before he opens the door. He's thinking something that he's not saying directly. Crystal sits a moment in the truck and then follows him inside the house. It's nice and cool compared with outside. A lazy cloud of flies floats over a little pile of dried cat shit on the vinyl floor. She wrinkles her nose. Dishes need to be caught up with. An orange and white cat lounges on top of the TV, another hides under the couch. In the kitchen and bathroom, sulphurous-smelling water drips from the taps, but the parched flies don't mind. "Just so you get the idea," Colin says and puts their overnight bags on the dining room table.

They have to park in the overflow lot, weave through cars, and push through crowds of people with strollers and kids with balloons. When they arrive at the trade show tent, Angus looks over her head and says to Colin, "I knew you'd be late. I can always count on that."

"It was my fault," Crystal says. She sells Avon, so she's learned a few ways of dealing with people. She reaches out her hand. Angus is a big guy with dark, curly hair and red cheeks. His eyes are lit with anger toward Colin. She steps forward, her body between the two of them, her hand still out. Angus notices her then. He takes her hand and pumps it. His hand is fleshy and calloused. She holds it until she feels him calm down, and then the three of them unpack the rest of the oils and creams and set them on the fold-up tables Angus has brought. On one side of them, a vendor is selling a drain-unplugging device, and on the other, they're offering samples of peanut brittle. That's good, Crystal figures; the peanut brittle will slow folks down.

"I need a beer," Angus says, and Colin says, "Sure. Go on."

In the first two hours, she and Colin sell more than two-hundred dollars' worth because Colin walks into the aisle with a confidential attitude and confesses that one jar of emu oil cream cured his foot fungus, but maybe the pretty lady doesn't want to see that, but take a look at his little gal. He nods toward Crystal, who stands and shimmies and waves. (They have devised this plan and his nod is her cue.) Angus-Pure Ranch Emu Oil cured the arthritis in her hips, and there she is, working the fair, bending her hips every which way.

People hand him cash and Crystal makes change. One old man buys a Hair Care Pak special for seventy-five dollars because Colin asks him, "You ever seen a bald emu?"

The man allows as he hasn't never seen an emu, and Colin says, "There you go," and makes the sale.

He comes back laughing, and Crystal says, "You con man," and kisses his whiskery chin. Then Angus joins them. He hands his dad some cash.

Crystal turns for her bag—her vitamins and antihistamines, her concealer and lip gloss—when Colin vanishes. The fact that he hasn't invited her to go with him makes her symptoms begin, like a car engine that cuts out, causes the car to roll to a stop. She and Angus sit in the booth. The peanut brittle vendor is on a break. The drain-opener fellow is dozing. Occasionally merry-go-round music bursts into the dark building. No one walks by.

Angus says, "I appreciate you coming. I'm good at growing the birds, rendering the fat, making the oil."

Crystal thinks about the word *rendering*. "You kill them?"

Angus nods. "I hate the selling part."

She touches the bottles—three ounces, six ounces, the pint specials, bulk-sized for the whole family—and thinks about the slaughter of emus. She hasn't thought about "emu oil," not precisely, thought maybe they had glands, like a cow, that gave out oil. She imagines the blood. Her battery blinks on low. She feels faint.

"Here." Angus passes her a flask. She sniffs the rye, hands it back. She'd nursed her alcoholic father, developed a taste for liquor herself. She remembers going to her first AA meeting, dirty bra strap showing. Angus hands her a Mars bar, and even though it's against her principles, she eats it.

"There's more to emus than their oil," Angus says.

She sips her negative-ion water and thinks Angus is suited to be a rancher, even one with unusual animals, because he has a slow rhythm. But when he speaks next, she feels the top of her head separate somewhere above her temples. The look on his face is secretive, angelic.

He says, "Emus are actually space creatures. They grant wishes."

"Grant wishes?" She reaches out and takes a customer's twenty dollars and says, "I guarantee this oil will help you," and hands over a three-ounce jar. People want miracles, that's plain.

"I've seen things out there in the pen with them."

She quips, "If emus could grant wishes, you'd have a wife to clean up that house of yours." The look on his big, shy face, the red flush, makes her wince. She says, "I hope God chokes me for saying that."

"I don't have much luck with women." He looks at his fleshy palms with their scars. "Figured I don't want a wife anyway. So it worked out."

"I'll see what I can do," she says, thinking of his house in need of help and those orange cats in need of litter box training.

Colin lost more than a hundred dollars in some game, and by the erratic way he's driving from the fairground to the ranch—he speeds up, slows down—and the tension in his jaw, she knows he's in a bad mood. Her heart goes crazy what with one thing and another, and the heavy heat in the truck doesn't help. Flat summer clouds silver the sky; lightning darts in the distance. Colin smokes a cigarette even though he's quit. Her eyes are raw, maybe from the smoke or an allergy, or the silence between them. The scent of grass and hay borne on the wind through the open window is strong. Angus in his old Chevy pickup isn't far behind. They pass through the gate of the Angus-Pure Ranch.

They land. That's how she feels when Colin jams the truck to a stop, slams the door, and leaves her sitting. She pats her skirt around her knees, looks out the windshield splattered with bugs. The mounds with horns out there would be the yaks. Or maybe the bison, she doesn't know. Brown-faced goats bleat in a pen near the house that needs paint. She sees all this. How to describe what happens next.

She drops down from the truck as though slipping through the sky. She descends and sinks right into the place. You turn, turn around, look at your life from wherever you're standing and that's where you are. These two men today are the only men she will ever need. An orange kitten rubs her leg.

She looks at the emus in their pen, clustered in the back. They elongate their necks and run at each other and ruffle their feathers. She watches them for a minute, looks at her feet in their flimsy sandals. You would never wear sandals like these if you lived on a ranch. She says out loud to no one, "I'm going in. I'm not afraid. You emus can pick lint off my shirt all you want."

And she's not afraid. Easy as pie, she works the latch and steps inside. One emu sees her. Then the others swivel their heads in her direction, and like a wave of feathers on stilts they come bobbing her way, their necks swaying from side to side, their eyelashes fluttering over heavy-lidded eyes, huge eyes. She hears deep-throated *bok-bok* sounds as they trample toward her, sounds like ping-pong balls hitting a table. They're so close, Crystal sees a whirlwind of dirt-pronged and scaly feet. Necks like fronds reach down for her. She ducks, puts her hands over her ears. Their beaks tap her neck, tap her skull, rip at her skirt. They pull her hair.

She hears Colin and Angus yelling. The men leap into the pen, arms and curses flying. The emus retreat like thunder. Colin draws her out.

Because she brought the wrong clothes, Colin gives her a pair of his jeans and Angus loans her a plaid flannel shirt. The shirt has been line-dried; it smells fresh and feels crisp on her skin. She joins Colin and Angus by the bonfire. After a while the three of them eat bison steaks under the stars. The animals shuffle around and bleat or grunt. Her heart stays where it should be, not losing its beat, not banging around to get out.

Before bed, she finds a well-used spatula in the kitchen, heads to the guest room, and flips cat shit out the open window. She tucks the spatula under the kitchen sink so no one will use it for scrambled eggs. As she steps carefully back to her room, she thinks that Colin's golden retrievers would like living on a ranch. Then she lies down on the covers, dabs her bruises with emu oil, and makes her wish.

South of Elfrida

They're on a birdwatching fieldtrip, driving only as far as Elfrida, through the unpopulated grids north of Bisbee, Arizona, up and down country roads, past flat, shorn grain fields, checking telephone wires and the tops of poles for raptors—hawks and falcons, eagles and kites. The landscape looks to Jean like Saskatchewan after harvest. She and two other women are crowded in the back seat of a white Camry driven by John Malcomb, the workshop leader, the tall, authoritative man Jean thinks of as "the hawk man." The temperature is soaring, but he won't use the air conditioning because a good birder needs to hear as well as see. Dust gusts in periodically through the open windows. Norma, the fourth woman in the car, is in the passenger seat keeping a tally of the birds they identify. At the morning lecture in the motel rec room, Jean assumed that Norma, passing out the doughnuts, was the hawk man's wife, but she's a regular, like some of the others, taking classes with him every chance she gets.

The three vehicles following are connected to the lead car by walkie-talkie. When the Camry pulls over, they pull over. Everyone quietly piles out, no slamming doors. They huddle over their birders' guides while the hawk man sets up his scope. Everyone must have a turn looking through the scope, and they guess and are wrong and guess again. And through his persuasive suggestions regarding the size of the bird in the air compared with the size of known objects (the width of a barn, the height of a telephone pole) and considering size and colour related to distance and distortion, adding in light and cloud and, so far as Jean can tell, adding willy-nilly flicks of colour here and there, all eventually agree with the hawk man and climb into the cars again. As the day passes, they troll by so many hardscrabble ranches, faltered land developments, trailers on half-acres, and half-started houses that Cochise County, Jean muses, will never amount to much property tax.

After a pit stop and quick lunch at a convenience store, Diane, the freckle-faced, small-boned woman on Jean's left, introduces the topic of cats, and they idly talk about cats in relation to birds. Jean hasn't told her fellow birders about her own cat, Buster Furman, back in the camper parked behind the motel, basking in the breeze from the Fantastic two-way fan. Buster Furman is seven years old and has been known to catch a few birds. "Tails," she tells him. "Tails, not feathers," but he has his limitations.

Norma glances over her shoulder at the group in the back seat. She bites her lip and then says, "I killed my neighbour's cat." The car grows so still you can hear the tires sweat on the surface of the road.

"How could you?" Jean sits forward.

"It saved the birds around my feeders."

"But it was someone's pet."

"I know. I heard the family calling him. I felt terrible. I had to pretend I didn't know anything."

Jean wonders out loud how Norma did it—the gruesome details—but the hawk man interrupts. "The damage to birds in North America cannot be calculated. The domestic cat is a killer, and no science can change the way they are."

"Yes," says Norma. She's thick-bodied, her hair a fading blond that, Jean knows, she'll have to make a decision about soon—cut it, colour it, or let it hang in greyish wisps, the sort of decision necessary beyond a certain age. Jean herself is beyond that certain age, on the cusp of fifty, and even as she tells herself she's willing to grow old, in an ideal world she doesn't want to do it alone, which may explain why, she thinks, she put up with her last boyfriend for so long.

"Each outdoor cat is responsible for the death of ten birds a year. And that's not counting feral cats," the hawk man says.

The women on either side of Jean nod.

Jean knows the statistics—seventy million cats in North America are born in the wild. Feral cats endure horrible lives—they breed, fight, starve, or freeze to death in the winter. Jean jumps at the chance to shift the conversation away from pets. She says, "Feral cats should be captured and euthanized."

"I don't like killing," murmurs Diane.

Jean knows the SPCA policy regarding feral cats—trap, neuter, return. "Returning neutered cats to their colonies doesn't save birds, does it? We are trying to save birds, right?" She feels righteous using *we*, as though she's a member of a principled club. She glances at the rear-view mirror. The hawk man isn't looking at her.

The car falls silent.

They drive slowly past another alfalfa field. Norma points. "Zone-tailed. Wow. Left."

"Where?"

"Eleven o'clock. Left."

"Why can't you describe where? Which pole?" He brakes.

"Flying. To the left of the hay barn. Eleven o'clock."

"Hell. That's a turkey vulture." The car lunges forward.

Jean wonders if the others are also wracking their brains for something to say. She murmurs, "Easy to confuse." He'd said so himself at the lecture.

You want to feel loathing move from one human being to another? Feel the disgust palpating from him in the driver's seat to her—*to me*, thinks Jean, squashed in the middle.

"At least we can count it," says the heavy-set woman on Jean's right, helpfully. "That's twenty-two turkey vultures today."

"What time is it now?"

"Two."

"We still have another three hours."

They drive on.

Jean sees a thin brown cow. Not a cow. A steer. A member of the cattle family, as the old man she'd met in California clarified. She lets her mind drift and imagines people in this environment keeping bees and making honey in sheds using plastic buckets, or putting their hopes into scrawny steers, animals that pick through the bristly landscape, future dinners on the hoof.

The workshop is based in a motel surrounded by barbed wire and warning signs in Spanish: PROHIBIDO EL PASO. NO HAY AQUA. Keep out. No water here. After choosing a space for the camper and hooking up to water and electricity, Jean strolled out beyond the iron gate—a sign said management locked the gate at 9:00 PM—to take a look around. She was grateful for the sunshine and heat. She'd had such a rotten time in California, she anticipated this workshop would be a holiday. The weather was holding, and best of all, she wasn't required to make decisions, she wasn't responsible for any of it, she was along for the ride.

The desert at the border consisted of coarse reddish dirt out of which struggled brushy scrub, low-lying thorny cactus, and a shiny line of border surveillance towers. She imagined bored men trapped inside, peering through binoculars. She thought of waving, thought again. The guys in there would be the new recruits, young, mouths teeming with insulting language toward women. She trotted back to the camper, cuddled with Buster Furman, read her paperback mystery, set the alarm.

At 6:30 AM eleven birders materialized and settled at tables in the motel's recreation room. After brief introductions, the lecture started. The hawk man—John Malcomb—was lanky yet powerfully compressed; his body looked taut, controlled, tough, and durable. Jean was impressed by his organization, the slides whipping by, the unwavering laser pinpointing what they should look for to positively identify the species and age of a bird. The precision in his presentation reminded her of the military, reminded her of her father. "Hawks," he told them, "are, strictly speaking, buteos." Jean liked that crisp, confident remark. He said they were to look for wrist commas, cheek colour, malar stripes. *Wrist commas, cheek colour, malar stripes.* Jean felt part of something wonderful there in that dingy room, the refrigerator grumbling. Wrists are at the bend of the wing, the cheek is the space below the eye, the malar the line below the beak—she could remember that. Clues to identification were subtle, he said. Location, light, and wind conditions could factor in. They weren't to leap to conclusions. The default hawk was a redtail unless they had a positive diagnostic field mark.

"It's a privilege to be with him," the woman sitting next to her whispered. "He is such an expert in the field." Jean, chewing on a day-old doughnut, had looked at the man again.

During the quick multiple-choice quizzes following a series of slides, Jean did well. She felt the hawk man's sharp eye settle on her, and she thought his lips moved in a smile, or something like a smile. A pleasant little flurry of feeling ruffled around in her chest; she was pretty sure he had taken note of her. He didn't look anything like her tailored, military-mannered father—this man was wearing a red kerchief around his neck, for one thing, and he had sandy hair and weathered skin—but she understood something about him because she knew her father. Her father had an even-tempered exterior belying a demanding core. Even though he wasn't a big man, you wanted to belong to his army; Jean certainly had. She had tried. When she heard the tone of quietly controlled loathing in the hawk man's answer to a woman's question, it was a tone at once faintly familiar and subtly thrilling. When they broke into groups to use the fewest vehicles, Jean had manoeuvred into the Camry. She told herself she'd learn more that way.

Jean had broken up with her long-time live-in boyfriend because she was tired of supporting him. He'd moved out, a little faster than she thought he would; she'd expected more of a battle. Then she'd drifted around the house, collected the rest of his things, and dutifully, decently, she'd thought, taken them to his new address, where, to her surprise, a woman answered the door. Jean was acquainted with her, a widow who worked in the library. He was living in another woman's house. Already. Behind the other woman's back, he blew her a kiss.

People would be talking, but she wouldn't be home to hear them. She signed up for winter birding workshops thousands of miles away from the reminder of what an idiot she was. Her first birding destination was the wildlife refuge at the Salton Sea, where there was a birding festival, with lectures on inland gulls and an owling field trip and group dinners. Jean signed up for everything, then spent half an hour on the phone with Ellie, who worked at the Blue Haven RV Park in Calipatria, California, not far from the Salton Sea. Ellie told Jean that Blue Haven was small and quiet, had some residents, nice people—Jean's kind of place. Jean had booked for three days, sight unseen, partly because Ellie confided that her father had just died and they'd then talked about fathers. Jean hadn't mentioned that hers was a colonel in the US Army; you never knew how people would react, though Ellie sounded like, as her father used to say, a friendly. Jean looked forward to having tea with Ellie and talking about things that mattered.

She crossed the border and drove south for nearly a thousand miles, through ice storms, snow, and sleet, until warmth broke out an hour north of Las Vegas, where there seemed to be a weather demarcation, as she'd posted on Facebook from the campground computer. She kicked off her boots, dug out her sandals. But two days later, entering California, torrents of rain pounded the windshield as she drove the last three hundred miles, Buster Furman hiding under the back seat, to the Blue Haven RV Park, where everything continued to go wrong.

She ran through the downpour to the office, a modular bungalow, and, opening the door, was assaulted by the aroma of air-freshening lilacs and a loud blast of talk TV. A black Lab, grey around the muzzle, settled in the walk-through space between public and private, gave her a sad-eyed look, sighed, and placed his snout back on his paws. Jean sniffed. What was that stink?

The TV went mute. Maybe the big woman sighing and flipping the register around for her to sign wasn't a good house-keeper. Maybe the old dog had intestinal issues. "You must be the one who called from Canada."

"I am! Are you Ellie?"

"Ellie's off today. We take only cash here. The ATM is outside. Three days' advance."

The back of Jean's neck stiffened. "Well, what if I don't stay three days?"

"Three-day advance. We don't take road trash."

"Oh." Jean had been singing "My Blue Heaven" and replacing the word *heaven* with *haven* for hours. She couldn't give up now. She put her credit card away. Twenty-dollar bills vanished from her hand.

After she parked on the slab of concrete under a little roof, she carried Buster Furman over her shoulder and into the camper. "Let me scope everything out first," she told him. He looked at her, eyes narrowed, so that the white streak above his eyebrow called attention to itself. His whiskers twitched. "Don't be that way," she said. "Don't you remember the coyotes in Nevada? Would you want to go through that again?" Buster Furman seemed to remember and jumped up on the bed.

She imagined she was living the life of an Alice Munro character, but her life in the camper—it was not a camper, it was a travel trailer, but the term *travel trailer* made it seem as though it could move on its own—was not like being on a ship with one's aunt sailing to Europe, or like being held captive to love and the subtle evilness of a man. Jean had simply chosen badly.

Where was the awful odour coming from? She lifted the lid of the Thetford toilet and sniffed. It was fine. She swung back outside.

An old man sitting in a lounge chair that had seen better days waved a cane at her from the porch next door.

She called, "Do you smell that?"

"No. I've been here too long to notice. It's a friendly place."

"What do you mean, too long to notice?"

He shifted his cane from one hand to the other. A green parrot squawked from a cage on the porch. "That's Petey. He's been with me since the wife died."

"Good," said Jean. "You've been here too long to notice what?"

"The feedlot." He pointed his cane.

"You mean those cows down the road?" Jean stepped closer.

"*Cows,*" he said and shook his head, chuckling. "You hear that, Petey? Cattle are cattle."

"Yuh, well." Jean had learned to add a soupçon of doubt in her *yuh well.* She felt sorry for an old man talking to a bird.

"You get used to it. It's a friendly place."

It took her a minute to connect the dots. She had never thought of thousands of animals lock-stepped together, a mud hole of packed, doomed beef—cattle, whatever they were. How could they not get sick, living as they did, up to their bony knees in mud and shit? No wonder they were fed antibiotics.

In stories where you could flip from one scene to another, skipping the awkward parts where the character doesn't know *where the hell* or *what the hell,* the reader could move a blank space or two and be in another scene, where the action starts again. The chesty woman at the desk of Blue Haven would not give Jean her money back. She spent a weepy hour driving away from that horrible place, through intermittent rain showers, to find somewhere safe to overnight and reconnoitre. At a sprawling RV park, a man at the security gate with CHUCK written on his shirt said he could give her a space for one night, but it wouldn't have a view. The sun was setting, spreading orange disintegration into the grey of the flattened rain clouds.

In the lead car, Jean is feeling tired, still in the picture but muted. She's not called attention to herself but she's been attentive. The hawk man drives and looks, drives and looks. "There," he says, spotting a speck on a telephone line in the distance, "is a juvenile red morph—" and then he's off, chasing it with his intelligence, his knowledge. He's visibly excited at sightings of the more splendid aerial predators. She understands that his mind fastens to their bodies and their predatory nature, she knows that he soars and dives along with them. Jean sees that he hunts with his eyes, hears his excitement every time he cries, "Do you see it? Do you see it?" She gets that he genuinely wants to share with them, and this touches her.

At the next stop—Harris's hawks—a couple from Tucson announces they're leaving; they have prior commitments for the evening. They hand over the walkie-talkie set. Birders in the second car take the opportunity to excuse themselves. Jean, standing slightly apart from the group, doesn't quite make up her mind in time—she half imagines herself leaving, but it would be awkward to ask them to wait while she grabs her stuff. The two vehicles flee. Jean thinks about Buster Furman in the camper and feels a tug of longing for him. She sips the last of her water, warm in her mouth.

The hawk man walks over, leans in, his big hand touching her waist. He smells dusty and leathery. "Can you imagine having anything better to do than looking at these magnificent creatures?" She shakes her head in agreement. He tells her to come look again through the scope to note the detail on the breast of a juvenile Harris's, perched on a post.

The women exchange brief smiles as they fold back into the Camry. Virtue is in the air; they're hanging in, they're not shallow, they're not like the others. Then Diane gets scalded: "Merlin!" she cries, and the man booms, "No, it is not!"

Something shifts for Jean then. They're like Mormon wives, these women, Jean thinks, these constant birders flying to distant places to repeat a workshop, signing on for more classes just to be badly treated.

"I have a cat." The admission sounds defiant. She hears her tone and hurries on. "My cat—Buster Furman—can't be kept indoors. His first owner tried, but—"

"You should still keep the animal inside. They get used to it." The hawk man's tone is decisive.

"But cats kept inside are weird. They get creepy. They prowl on the backs of sofas."

The flicker of movement in the corner of the man's mouth does not bode well. Through the rear-view mirror his eyes latch on to hers. "If you have a cat, you have a responsibility to keep it inside."

"My cat was born to hunt. He catches mice and other rodents," Jean says stubbornly, deliberately oblivious to the building energy and the covert looks the other women send him.

His foot hits the accelerator.

Jean falls into herself, brooding. Her boyfriend was soft and malleable; he had no aims or goals in life, sometimes needed help getting through the day. The hawk man would always get through his day and survive anything—sand fleas in south Texas, deer ticks in Nebraska, biting beetles in Australia. He would survive swamps or smells in whatever terrain he chose to stride through, scouting the species he has the most affinity for, the species he admires. He names, sorts, counts, *bags them*, she thinks, the buteos, the accipiters, the hawks—he bags the birds, each one a bride. She recognizes the intensity in him, the coldness. She craves his focused energy; she wants in.

When they rise over the next small hill and begin the slow, searching descent, she glances up and sees him looking at her. A penetrating look. It's hard to tell what his intention is, but something might be going on. He's handsome and commanding. She gives a half smile.

Thinking of the cat that belonged to Norma's neighbour, Jean says, hedging, "The cat that Norma killed probably deserved it." As soon as the words are out of her mouth, she's mortified. Diane quickly looks away. Jean's motivation is so patently obvious. She's let herself be drawn into an act of treachery, as her father would say, and now she's losing ground.

In the rear-view mirror the hawk man's eyes fill with satisfaction.

She's caught in a tight spot in the back seat of that car. She flashes back to Buster Furman on his pillow beside her for those thousands of miles as she skittered on edges—through blizzards in Washington, the diesel truck that narrowly missed them in Idaho, roadside camping in Nevada, cloudbursts in California—and from beginning to end, Buster Furman displayed faithfulness and patience, as well as good listening skills. How could she have betrayed him? She imagines him, her own dear cat, scooped from her lap, tossed out the window, him and his purrs catapulted out of reach in the wind of the moving car, his tender paw pats on her cheek at dawn receding, him just hurtling along, trusting her in his loyal way, until all his beloved little seams—his armpits, his extra toes, his ears—are swept into the talons of a raptor and are gone.

Stronghold

*

Just back from a recent trip to Indonesia, I went in for gallbladder surgery, picked up a hospital superbug, spent time in isolation, and nearly died. That's the long and short of it. The series of events happened so fast, and were so unexpected, that it seemed impossible they were happening to a woman who was known by her associates as organizationally anal-retentive. The experience was like driving down a summer road and being caught up in a tornado, the sort of thing you read about. Afterwards, roaming through the rooms of my glorious house on its hill in Boulder, I paused at this particular lovely ceramic or that remarkable painting; the house was crammed with exquisite rugs, wall hangings, trinkets, and crafts. Su-Zee Imports sold items to retailers in the western states, and there was a little warehouse on the property as well that employed four people in packing and shipping. "Not because I've lost my mind along with my gallbladder," I told my long-time friend Myrna on the phone, "but because my whole fucking life is here, in things. What was I doing all those years?"

"Making money," Myrna said.

I laughed and hung up, lay down, got up again—it hurt—and continued to cruise through and admire the house. Everything about it was mine—I'd designed it, chosen the architect, the woodworkers, and the painters. I scoped out the kitchen with its immaculate counters and shiny stovetop; between that and the untouchable look of zero-landscaped grounds, the house felt unlived in. Most of my life, I saw, had been lost in a business coma—driven, successful, and lonely as hell.

I called again. "What is it with gallbladders?"

"Hold on." Myrna was tapping on her keyboard. "Gallstones mean bitterness, hard thoughts, pride."

"Thanks for bucking me up." Then I told her that since the damn surgery I had the urge to sell everything, get rid of it all.

"Don't do anything rash," Myrna counselled. "Get a dog."

A dog? What in the world would I do with a dog? I tried to picture one, came up with a Rottweiler with bared teeth. "What's bugging me is the pain in my missing gallbladder. The doctor says it's a phantom pain, impossible. He's prescribing anti-spasm pills and telling me to eat soup."

"Love heals. You need something to love and a change of scenery. I'm having a Blue Moon Ceremony, second full moon in November. We'll be calling in the mountain spirits. The Apache warrior Cochise himself, if I'm lucky."

"And I'm destined to be there? The planets are aligned in my chart?"

"Some gals from the ranch will be over. Bring the dog."

"What the hell."

Myrna had made a dramatic move from the East Coast to Arizona, parked herself in the Dragoon Mountains that she raved about. I imagined her house, made from real adobe bricks using dirt from the land (she'd made a big deal about it), with terra cotta-coloured concrete floors (that she'd sanded herself) and solar panels on the roof; her decor would be minimal—a Navajo rug here, a piece of Western art there—because Myrna valued austerity.

I decided to try a change and had my hair dyed a dark purple-burgundy and tightly curled, so that with a band fastened around the top, I looked like a white woman's take on an African Zulu, a look that suited my tanned skin and long cheekbones. Next, after investigating puppies, I bought a purebred teacup poodle, a little guy with black curls and intelligent chocolate eyes, and named him Baby. Why not call him Baby? I'd missed out on having a child.

The breeder gave instructions that Baby needed to be with me night and day, so he would grow up calm and collected; the world was new to him, and I would be his comfort. Fine by me. Baby was responsive for something so small, adaptive, and willing, easy to train. Having him trekking behind, following me around the house, his little paws tapping on the tiles, made me smile as I went about complying with the doctor's orders, mincing vegetables for soup.

Of course I decided to go to Myrna's, and it worked out that a faithful employee, a wealthy gal from Connecticut, was delighted to carry on with managing Su-Zee Imports. "You can borrow our Roadtrek for your trip. Dave would love to demonstrate how it works."

The Roadtrek was slightly bigger than a van and had all the amenities of a miniature home—a dining table, a TV, an armchair, and a double bed. Dave showed me how to manage the toilet and the water system—which hoses to use to dump "grey water" and "black water" (disgusting), and where they were stowed—how to light the pilots for the hot water tank, the furnace, the cook stove, and the refrigerator. It was a compact little world, and once again I thought, *What the hell*.

Boulder was lightly dusting itself with snow when we set out. Baby found his place on the passenger seat and seemed contented just to be close. We drove west on the I-70 into Utah and camped two nights in Moab, near Arches National Park, in canyon country. "What have I been missing all these years?" I asked Baby. Having travelled all over eastern Asia for business, I'd missed seeing the locally beautiful places. Baby was happy in a dog-carrier backpack on walks. Other times, he liked being on his leash so he and his black velvet rhinestone collar could be admired. To avoid snow in the Utah high country, we detoured down through Navajo lands, dropping from Flagstaff to Phoenix, losing altitude along the way. Sometimes, on a steep hill, Baby would run from the front of the van to the back and then tumble on the carpet like a little ball to land near my feet.

On the last overnight before reaching Myrna's, I steered into the sort of place you choose on your way to somewhere else, a campground with twelve rough sites out in the open and no hookups for anything except water. In the shaggy eucalyptus trees, black birds—grackles—squeaked and whistled. When choosing the spot, I wasn't sure if the noisy birds overhead were a good sign, and later wished I'd paid attention to that inner alarm. But it was four in the afternoon, the hottest time of day in that part of Arizona, and besieged by the damn pain, I slid open the panel door, hoping for some relief from the heat. Just then, Baby threw up on the carpet runner and I shrieked. He seemed to fly out the open door, only to be hit by a fifth-wheel backing in to park beside me.

I remember I yelled, "Oh, no!" instead of his name. A man with a straggly growth of white beard stepped down from the cab. "Upon my grave, I am so sorry," he said and clambered back in to pull forward. By then, seeing Baby's tiny shattered body, my blood sugar took a dive. The man's wife, wearing sunglasses with polka dot frames, brought an aluminum chair for me. She faced it away from where Baby lay.

The skinny old man's eyes were a watery hazel, and his wrinkled green T-shirt advertised, MUSTANG RANCH. The wife had those retro sunglasses. I can recall these details but can't focus on what Baby looked like in general, whether the white tuft of fur was on his left paw or his right paw. The man said, "I'm an ordained born-again preacher, so your little fella is in good hands." I heard the sound of a shovel scraping, the sound of digging. It was scrubland country, high and dry, with low-growing thorny things gripping the dirt. Then he called me to the service.

"The service?"

At the woman's voice interrupting my story about Baby, I look around the patio at the group of five women gathered for the Blue Moon Ceremony, their faces ruddy from the wind that whips up in the Dragoon Mountains nearly every day, so Myrna says. They wear jeans and gobs of turquoise jewellery and cowboy boots. They've driven Dodge pickups or SUVs to Myrna's and give one another looks as they listen to me, the old friend, the stranger with the weird purplish hair, tell the story about the death of her little dog. I'd told Myrna essential bits when I'd arrived, and then ignored her touchy-feely questions, pleaded exhaustion. Now I can't seem to shut up. In the background Myrna moves nimbly between the house and the patio. I've kept an eye on the changing light on the mountains behind the women in the semicircle of chairs while recounting Baby's story. The woman asking the question about the service is a hefty gal in her forties with a tattoo of roses around her right ankle. Myrna places chips in a blue bowl on the table. She says, "Baby was a yogi."

"Yogi?"

"A being that teaches you about yourself."

Myrna is annoying just now. Baby was a dog. "The service," I say, getting back to the story. "Remember I told you the man said he was an ordained preacher. So, yeah, the graveside service."

Someone's radio was singing country blues, a forlorn love song. Two kids from a nearby campsite scattered pebbles on the grave. The little girl, her feet wiggling in pink flip-flops, sniffled. The brother whispered, "Shut up, snot face." The preacher and his wife lowered their heads and pressed their palms, fingers to the sky. "God bless this little fella. May this little fella rest forever in the arms of his Maker." His hands shook. Then he made the sign of the cross. That gesture—the sign of the cross—did it for me. No real born-again would touch that symbol.

I lean forward, palms on thighs, elbows akimbo, and run my eyes past each woman. Their expressions become wary, as though I am unpredictable, which maybe I am. I lower my voice. "Let me tell you what I felt. I felt a cold, stabbing hatred toward that man. And I still do." A bat flits by. I flick a hand before resuming. "I told him he owed me two thousand bucks."

"You actually said that to him?"

Eyes narrowed, I look steadily in the direction of the woman asking. After the so-called burial, I left the campground, drove into town, and parked under a streetlight in front of a drugstore to wait for daylight, then drove like a maniac to get to Myrna's. Now all I'm getting is flack.

Myrna emerges from the house carrying a basket of sound-makers on her hip, and states, "Bats are good luck, by the way. They mean a departed spirit is listening. And, yes, she did say that. Those very words. 'You owe me two thousand bucks.' Teacup poodles are expensive." Myrna has long, Pocahontas-black hair, shiny and straight, with an illegal eagle feather tucked into a leather sweatband. She hands a shaker with fur decoration to the woman who spoke. "We used to call these rattles. They are not rattles—kids use rattles. These are shakers. You don't rattle them, you swish them back and forth, like a tide. This one is made from turtle shell." She gives out two gourd shakers. "The relationship between Suzanne and her little dog was in the formative stage. She'd only had him for less than a month."

I pull my knees up, rest the heels of my clogs on the edge of the chair cushion. "The old shit gave me fifty dollars."

Pink wisps of clouds move through the deepening blue.

Someone murmurs.

"What?"

"To put a price on love."

Thank God the bottle of tequila is coming my way. At least these strangers and I have one thing in common—the hope of getting smashed. I reach for my shot glass. "It was a matter of principle." I'm determined to make my point between pouring and gulping, throat burning. "Besides, I didn't love Baby. Not yet."

"Love takes time." Myrna hands out a rain-stick and some leather bells. "Being sexually impulsive, I've learned that lesson the hard way." She flutters into the house.

The women laugh and glance at one another and wait for Myrna to return. This time she's lugging a tall cowhide drum. She places the drum next to me and gazes toward the mountains. "The Moon goddess is on her way. This is a night for dreams, insight, a night for truth. She has gone to a lot of trouble to bring us into her consciousness."

Someone starts to make a joke—maybe a joke about the hard-working moon—and stops. Someone else giggles. Faces are less distinct; the light is disappearing as the moon brightens a cleft in the mountains. Myrna takes her seat, uses her knuckles to hit the stretched hide surface of her hand drum, then swishes an open hand over the top, the sound like sifting sand. Everyone seems still, watching and waiting. Breathing in, what I inhale is tension, so I say, "Do you want to hear more about my dead dog?" No one laughs. Myrna's hand sweeps the drum's surface. "'I have arrived in heaven.' This is a quotation from Cochise. Imagine him here. Imagine his suffering, his stalwart resistance, the truths he had to face. He said, 'I am alone in the world . . . I have drunk of the waters of the Dragoon Mountains and they have cooled me. I do not want to leave here.'"

Feet shuffle. Someone kicks a stone.

Myrna whispers, "Let she who needs to speak do so."

My thought is, *She must make up these lines on the fly.*

The woman with the rose tattoo says, "Okay, I'll start. I steal money from my husband's wallet. He doesn't have a clue. I feel like a kid, the cookie jar thing."

"Revenge," someone offers.

"Revenge?"

I recognize a defensiveness similar to my own and pipe up, "Yeah, well. Revenge for making her live out here in this hellhole."

Now they laugh. It's getting dark enough so that their faces meld into the warming orange colours the mountains throw into the violet sky. Myrna's drum stops and we're quiet. I reach for another shot of tequila.

A small voice says, "Me, I had an affair. It was early on so don't bother mentioning it to him now." A ripple of laugher runs around the circle. In between each story there is silence. Bells jingle, gourds comment.

Myrna motions that I should stay seated and hold the cowhide drum between my thighs. She demonstrates how to use the beater, a wooden stick wrapped in deer leather, then stands, holding her hand drum ready. Everyone rises and forms a semicircle facing the mountains.

Myrna calls out, "Mountain spirits, Moon goddess, hear us." She hits her drum. One, two, three, thirteen times. As the moon rises, Myrna begins to chant. Her voice, warbling deep in her chest, sounds eerie and so strong that the vibration thumps through the bones in my own chest. I bang the powwow drum, listen to Myrna, and soon get the rhythm and even give the singing a try. As the moon becomes a yellow globe, we're chanting, "Way ha, way ya, ya hey ya hey, wah hey ya hey wah hey yo."

In the no-man's land between sleep and wakefulness, voices speak languages I don't understand. Images of people I don't know flash by. It isn't the fault of the bed, I conclude toward morning; it was the damn moon. At home, I always hide from a full moon because if it spots me, it influences my sleep or dreams; I've always known it. Last night the full moon saw me all right— she was in full view and, daring fate, I stood before her.

Myrna makes Bloody Marys for breakfast, adds a spoonful of canned green chiles to the eggs as she scrambles them. "If Cochise hadn't run out of Mexican horses to steal or lived in another century, he would have laughed at us last night. God. The energy here is so confusing. You saw the local gals."

I catch the toast and butter it. "Mmm. I thought they were down with it."

Myrna says, "Down with it? They're posers. Doesn't matter how much turquoise you wear. They're just skimming the surface. They want something they've never had before, and this is what we do."

"Who are they? Knitters?"

"Weight watchers. Collectors of photos of grandchildren. I couldn't get my Yay ha way ha's straight." Myrna takes the plate of bacon from the microwave. "When I lived in the east, I took lessons from a Cree singer. The singing's syllabic, but you can tell the real from the fake. We were just wailing, making fools of ourselves."

"It had a certain synergy."

Myrna laughs.

Nibbling toast, parts of the dream come to mind. "I had a crazy stupid night. There was woman wearing a really strange hat. She had a message for you."

Myrna cuts the crust off a piece of toast, tears the crust into pieces, and places them one at a time into her mouth.

"I think you'd call my dream a real honest-to-God New Age dream."

Chewing slowly, Myrna raises her eyebrows.

"You don't think I'm capable of having a message dream?" No, actually, she doesn't, but I plow on. "You don't want to know about the hat?" Myrna loves hats; she'd had a good business designing hats.

"If you insist."

"The hat was wide-brimmed, decorated with feathers."

"You mean a hat from the Victorian era, with stuffed larks and warblers?"

"In my experience, in Arizona the birds would be grackles."

Myrna gives me a look and tosses her hair over her shoulders.

"The woman was stately, tall, proud. She said you really want to make love to an Indian and maybe you loved an Indian in another life, she isn't sure." I know I sound like a simplistic idiot. I tear up the last of my toast and imitate her and delicately place it piece by piece in my mouth.

Myrna suddenly becomes busy, brushing crumbs into her hand, spinning around the kitchen. I recognize that these are evasive moves on her part and wait, licking my fingers. She turns on the tap, adds detergent, looks over her shoulder at me. "Those women last night were packing. It's strange living out here. Usually they put their guns on the kitchen counter. Last night . . ."

Okay, so she wants to change the subject. I'm willing to humour her. "Guns? Come on."

"Their husbands are mostly ex-military. Look around. It's lonely. What do we have, realistically? Some free-ranging cattle, houses acres apart, illegals walking through. The war on drugs has escalated the violence, brought in organized gangs. Eyes are everywhere."

I think about eyes. A creamy mound of scrambled eggs calls out. I stab it with my fork. "Baby watched everything I did."

Myrna collects her plate and the cooking pans and slides them into the sink. "Think of it this way. Baby was like the weather balloon near the border. It only looks like a weather balloon; it's really a spy camera, and now, in your case, it's gone."

"Damn, I hate you." Snatching the last piece of bacon, I open my mouth, snap my jaws.

Myrna plans to drive us into the Coronado National Forest, adjacent to the ranch, to the hideout used by Cochise. After the breakfast feast, we dress accordingly: long sleeves and light-weight pants that tuck into hiking boots. This hideout isn't the famous one, the stronghold on the east side, where the Chiricahua Apaches and their families eluded the US Cavalry for so long, she tells me as we pack a cooler with sandwiches, pasta salad, bottles of water, and wine into her SUV. "I'm taking you to the real hideout, the place the men lived, the warrior braves, when their freedom was lost and they knew it." She heaves the trunk shut. "And I haven't forgotten your dream. I'm thinking about it."

At the gate she punches in four numbers on the security box; we pass over a cattle grate, and she hops out to shut the gate. "One time I found hunters in here. In a nature sanctuary! They were wearing camouflage gear. Beer and rifles. They were not Border Patrol taking a break."

I admire the way Myrna rants, as she always did, this time expressing incredulity that anyone would even think of trespass-ing into a nature sanctuary, much less do it.

Soon we enter the opening of a canyon where oaks, junipers, and manzanitas are watered by a creek. The mountains' flat breaks, like stacks of crispy bread, and the lichen on the granite that make the reddish rock appear pistachio green or like rinds of lemons are stunning. As we grind along a gravel road about as wide as a walking trail, I hold the Thermos of coffee away from my lap. My hair brushes my face, retreats, brushes, retreats; I like the wiry, overprocessed feel.

"Cochise was a Chiricahua Apache. The Chiricahua were different from the Apaches to the east. In the long run, retaliatory raids against the army were futile, but Cochise knew Doomsday was coming." Myrna is in her anthropology professor mode, her first career. "The man was mythic in his capacity to vanish. You won't see the place until we practically fall into it."

The morning blue of the sky shifts to greys that look heavy, weighed down; in Colorado I'd be thinking snow. The road is disintegrating into washboard; we bounce, and things rattle around in the back. I remove my sunglasses, place them on the seat. Myrna is still talking about Cochise, but I don't mind. My friend is obsessed, and there's that past life to consider.

Myrna says, "I do love it here, and I would like to stay. Sometimes, though, this solitude scares me. Then I decide that fear is necessary for an interesting life. Then I go so far as to think I wouldn't be apprehensive if I had a man around."

"With your luck, you'd have to take care of him." I speak reflexively, forgetting Myrna's second husband, who was great-looking but a gambler. It cost her a fortune to get out of that one.

The SUV veers as the right front tire hits a rock. "Shit," she says.

"I didn't mean it that way. Oh, hell."

"Mean what?"

When my skull knocks against the passenger window, she takes her foot off the pedal. "Sorry."

I touch my temple, check for a lump, mull over an angry response, then consider one that's prim or even pitiful—I can go there—but laugh instead. "You are such a brat."

We pass a standing pool of water where sycamore and sagebrush exchange black-throated sparrows, the birds made flighty by the car. I remember Baby's little brown eyes, his butt-wiggling when he snuggled in my arms. "Baby licked my chin but not my face." I mention it as though the behaviour was a virtue. "He was cute."

"You loved him. Case closed."

Being the good friend that I am, I press my lips tightly together—Myrna can be such a pain—turn my mind back to wondering about precipitation and the sky and whether it snows in Arizona at five thousand feet altitude this far south and why, despite all Myrna's explanations, I don't know much about where I am, though I sense running all around me—rabbits, or quail, or something else in the deep canyons, chased by coyotes with narrow faces and piercing eyes.

"Damn." Her voice makes me jump. "I missed the turn. We're too far south. I tell you, if I didn't know this place existed, I'd never find it." The bottles clink in the cooler as she whips around.

I snort. "Well, it is a hideout."

"I wish you'd take this seriously. I am leading you to a spiritual moment."

In university we studied art history and fought the good fight in radical politics. We travelled in Eastern Europe before it was easy. Despite what I think about Myrna's attitude, one that borders on good-old-fashioned churchy rectitude trimmed with fur and feathers, the fact that we've know each other so long makes our friendship feel charmed.

"Here." She brings the SUV to a skidding stop, flings open the door, and bats her hat at the cloud of dust. "Wear your hat and put those sunglasses back on. The light will ruin your eyes."

I obey—"Whatever you say, oh leader"—and scramble out. She leads me along a crevice, so tight we turn sideways to slip through. I follow her as the crevice opens along a flank of rock, touching warm slabs as I pick my way upward through a winding, narrow canyon, low mesquite and grasses growing out of gravelly soil, until, as we climb to the right, a trail gradually appears and I find my feet stepping on flat rocks. I'm panting from exertion and take a moment to scan the width of the steps. "Cochise must have been tall."

"Fast," Myrna says. "Like wind." Her silhouette is dramatic against the sky; her black hair catches the sun and for a moment looks ablaze. I'm about to applaud but she turns and bounds upward and I have to pick up my pace, keep my eyes on the toes of my heavy boots, footwear unlike anything Cochise would have worn. Then she extends her hand and tugs me around some brushwood. I can't see an entrance until she tells me to duck and pulls me inside.

"Wow."

We stand listening to each other's breathing as we recover from the hike. The cave is bigger than I'd imagined it would be and smells cool and clean.

Myrna has been before, obviously, and, just as obviously, she has analyzed the three rooms. The one we're in must have been for sleeping, she says, because it's the most concealed and has no view. "The walls are polished, notice? As though men had nothing to do for long periods of time but chip rock, smooth it, and dream of the women left behind."

Discreetly I roll my eyes.

In the second room, I lose my footing and Myrna catches me, murmuring, "You can float away if you're not grounded." When I'm upright, she switches to tour-guide mode and swings her arms in a slow arc. "Don't you think this room would be perfect for supplies?" Again she reaches for my hand, this time to lead me to the entrance of a low passageway. "Keep your head down, eyes forward. I'll go first." We trundle, one at a time, through the darkness and emerge into a space, a horizontal fissure in the rock, like a clamshell open to the sky.

The vastness of the plain below—stippled with dwarf trees and dusty green brush and the occasional ocotillo cactus—is so astonishing, I am speechless.

Myrna says, "You are safe here. You can see everything."

She moves to one side and places her arms around a standing rock. The rock is odd because it's about four feet tall, and looks as though it's grey and white, a piece of granite—wrong time, wrong place.

She gestures for my attention. "Notice the hollow at the top. This would be a grain-grinding rock. Years of grinding corn into meal. Makes me wonder if a woman lived here." Now her mouth twitches. A glow seems to rise around her.

For a minute I stare hard at my friend, her features shyly veiled between the curtains of dark hair, before I get it, but I want her to be the one to say it. "And?"

She throws her head back with what I take to be some pride, as she displays her lovely throat and neck. She says, "Your dream suggests I was that woman, the woman who was not a wife. The woman who stayed for the warriors."

"Aha." I exhale the word as though I've triumphed. The lopsided grin on her face, a face that's seen a lot of years and a lot of sun, brings words to my lips. I hear myself say, "The Victorian dreamer, the collector of, well, she says they're priceless, the birds for her hats, thinks you're in love. She told me to tell you that you're in love." I have no idea what I mean, but as soon as the words are out, they seem plausible.

Myrna bows, pressing her hands palm to palm, and then she giggles—it's uncommon and unsettling to hear Myrna giggle—and says coyly, "Am I?" Then she falls into what I can only think is a ceremonial rendering of what she feels based on what I've said. I watch like someone at a private performance, the performer herself self-conscious, aware that I'm watching. Myrna lowers her arms to her sides, drops her head, and stands perfectly still. The silence streams through my mind like stars pulsing in a desert night. The words don't belong to me; what do I know about desert stars? She says, "Yes, I am in love. Don't laugh. I'm in love with a person who lived in another life. When you love, you're not alone. I am not alone." I notice the tiny spot at her crown where she was hit by a rock when she was a child.

I love the idea and want to follow her words all the way home. I, however, have no such feeling of being not alone; I feel like poorly made fabric about to unravel. My hands ache, miss sorting through textiles, intricately woven rugs, and cloth made almost entirely of beads, shells, and little pearls. I miss the markets, the bazaars, the noise and purposeful merriment of Malaysia.

"I want to live in these mountains," Myrna says. "I do not want to leave here." When she has held a few seconds of silence, she crosses her ankles and folds her body down to sit on the ledge. She rubs her hands along her upper arms as though to stop the shivers.

I sink into my own truth. What I want is not to sit on any ledge but stay as I am, hugging the wall. But if she's out there, I will be too. I take courage and lower myself on all fours, creep to the ledge, sit carefully, not letting my legs hang over as Myrna's are, and lean back on my arms. A hawk soars below us. "Redtail," whispers Myrna.

"How do you know?" The hawk sinks and rises as it plays with a current. Leaves on trees shielding the cave from below rustle. I say, hesitantly, "I feel disoriented. It's like we're invisible."

"We always have been. Welcome to earth." Myrna sounds far away.

A tremble of fear ripples in my belly. Images come fast and discouraging as I face what I did the day Baby was killed: "I yelled at him for throwing up. I cared about a fucking carpet."

Myrna's warmth is like a hand around my shoulders, though she herself seems held in place only by an aura. I hear her say, "Thank you for your dream. It is such a gift. As for you, your issue is pride. 'Through sorrow, pride is driven out.' And, hey, here's a message." She chortles. "Change your name to Harmony if it helps."

I give a moment to trashing everything Myrna values, search through rough, snarling-sounding words to flout everything she believes in—the drumming, the Moon goddess, revelation, messages bundled in messy dreams. Cynical remarks come to mind and then, in the time it takes to snap your fingers, I let them pass through, let them go, think, "Harmony." Peace descends. Under my hands I feel the silky tight curls of a wiggly little dog, and though I know Myrna has been leading me to an epiphany ever since I arrived in the Dragoon Mountains distraught and denying it, I miss Baby with all my heart. I love him, and knowing I love him, I soften, am laid bare, and cry. Flakes tumble, swirl in the wind, evaporate at the touch of rock.

The Compact

Sally and Al are in their blue canvas chairs, side by side, under the red-striped awning. An American flag flies on the permanent pole in front. Al—once a lieutenant in the paratroopers—won't have it any other way. Back when they travelled, wherever they went, he set up the flag, let it fly night and day, just to remind those left-wingers that they were desecrating the US of A with their fuzzy-headed ideas, welfare for every Tom, Dick, and Harry—God did not give a man hands if He didn't want a man to use them. Al's wife, Sally, has been by his side, gauging her remarks by the expression on his face—he can't abide a chatty woman—for twenty-five years. She's a second wife, hard as that is to believe considering all their years together, and she knows where she stands. The children he had by the first wife have turned out well—real estate, marketing—but their son together is the maintenance man of this very RV campground that calls itself a "resort." They stay here most of the year, in their gleaming thirty-four-foot Monaco La Palma, to keep an eye on him, to keep him sober and drug-free. They have the spot as close as they can get to his double-wide, sometimes go over with bread for the caged parrot on his porch and steak bones for his Doberman.

The bumper sticker on their Dodge Ram advertises Al's feelings: America, love it or leave it. Sally thinks he's stuck in the 1970s. But to each his own; she, too, has her flaws. She flosses her teeth in front of the TV. She rinses coffee cups without soap, just runs her fingers around the rims, dries them, and puts them away.

She likes it at this campground/resort—really nice folks from all over, and she's made friends with some of the wives. They knit or crochet together, sip rum and Cokes (what do the boys know) while they hang out at the pool. At the end of March the girls and their husbands leave, back to Wisconsin or Michigan, and the last of the bus-like diesel pushers pulls out, a little car hitched to the back, along for the ride. By then, the weather is really hot and if she didn't have prescription sunglasses, the sun would burn out her eyeballs. Thank goodness for air conditioning and her body's tolerance for heat.

In her opinion, not that anyone would ask, she and Al do a lot of sitting around. Al putters, polishes the rig, and tinkers with his truck while she crochets little nothings she donates to the Salvation Army. She can't bring herself to make something useful, like a sweater for a baby, so she makes doilies for old ladies who might need new ones. Her friends at the pool snickered when she made that comment.

Sometimes she thinks she'd like to volunteer somewhere, but the problem, from Al's point of view, is that Mexicans are everywhere, people who can't keep their fingernails or a toilet bowl clean unless they're paid to do it. She's been to the barrio, looked around. In Tucson these days it's hard to get out of the barrio; it's like the downtown has been taken over by aliens, that's Al's word for them, and white people—the people who founded the country—are pushed farther out, left sitting inside gates and fences in the middle of nowhere, just waiting for sunset. And something cold to drink, she can face that fact; you need something to drink out here with nothing to see but sky and the wind blowing dirt so hard she thinks the mountains will be smaller in the morning. Whatever's in the wind makes her nose tickle, her throat hurt. Allergies. Everybody in Pima County has allergies.

"Go get that box of tissues," he says. "I can feel you revving up." Him speaking that way makes her feel fond.

"About to have a sneezing fit," she says.

"Can count on that with this wind. You take that pill the doctor gave you?"

"Oh, it just makes me . . . oh, I don't want to say."

"Pee, woman, that's the word you're searching for."

"Oh, you," she says, batting his arm, stepping inside for that new box of extra soft, extra strong.

Through the screen door, Al says, "How about that meatloaf tonight."

Sally opens the fridge. "I thought pork chops."

"Got my heart set on meatloaf. Betcha there's a store up the road."

"Betcha you're right." She's used to his little demands. She has nothing else to do, not really. She plucks the car keys from their hook.

She drives up Kolb Road to Fry's. As soon as she's inside the glossy store, under the fluorescent lights, she sighs. The store is like a sanctum, the church she doesn't attend. She loves the privacy and peace. She pushes her cart to the meat aisle and meditates in front of the wrapped packages of ground beef.

Al was away at military training when she had the abortion. She couldn't have got it past him; the child would have been part black. She understands that, genetically, the child could have been very white or very black or something in between, but she couldn't take the chance. She wonders, dawdling in front of the meats, what that child would have been like— smart, maybe, different.

She had it done at a private clinic, away from the base. She'd asked that the tiny little thing be cremated; she keeps some of the ashes in a powder compact, the lid decorated with enamelled butterflies, jewels in their wings. A soft, pink powder puff covers the ashes. She keeps it in a drawer along with her many cosmetics, the lipsticks, foundations, eyeliners, and other women's necessities. Al never looks in this drawer; he'd rather not think about the effort she puts in, to look groomed and pretty.

Waiting at the checkout, she notices so many young people with all shades of skin colour. They're pretty, the girls with olive skin, long faces, dark hair, a little slant to the eye. God may never forgive her that sin. The price you pay—she paid— for a moment of freedom.

After fixing the meatloaf, Sally returns to her canvas chair with a second glass of wine, though Al doesn't need to know it's her second. Here comes a Class C Adventurer, passing carefully over the speed bumps. "A 2001," Al says. She pats his hand. He's always right on the money about the models. They look pretty much the same to her, but Al says that's because she's a woman.

Now here's something that causes them to share eye contact—two women together in the cab. Both of them have short brown hair, and Sally knows at first glance they ain't sisters. She suspects the new gal on duty in the office will let them stay for a night or two because most of the regulars are gone for the season—it being April—and there isn't an image to uphold. Al says, "Look at that. Should be against the law, letting people like that in here."

And she says, "Yes, it's a shame." She feels envy mixed with pity. Envy because not having a man to lord it over you would be a relief—every time she has this thought, she asks God's forgiveness—and pity because some women just fail at being women. Something wrong with that; she's certain. A woman needs a man, period. A good man is organized and keeps his world that way, even if she herself still chafes, acts out through dark, nasty little deeds. Just a few minutes ago, wrist deep in the muck of meat, eggs, and breadcrumbs, the little rebel in her rose up and she spit into the mixture.

Here come those two women, out of the office, both wearing beige shorts and white sport socks, showing off their muscular legs. How does God make so many variations on a theme? Sometimes it just takes the lives of others to make you grateful for what you have.

Mabel and Ed stop by in their golf cart decked out with American flags. The four of them look over at the Class C Adventurer, jockeying to park beyond the row of palm trees. "That is just a crime against human nature," Mabel says, and Al says, "You wanna Bud?" and so they pull in under the canopy and unfold chairs Al keeps at the ready. Sally slips inside for glasses and Al reaches into the cooler for the beer. In a moment, they're set.

The sky turns pimento red, a line of blue lavender above

it, and above that, a tender wash of pink, the colour of Sally's white Zinfandel. They watch stealth bombers returning to Davis-Monthan Air Force Base, the eastbound planes taking tourists home, and, to the south, the helicopters on border patrol. Sally nestles into her chair. Here she is, looking exactly like a person living quietly under the radar.

Banished

Stefan bites into his emu burger at a café in Tombstone. He looks across the table at Karen, her face lit from a window, the café curtains pulled back so customers can see the frontier townspeople passing by, garbed in long skirts and cowboy gear. The splotches where once Karen had acne are obvious. He knows she spends a fortune on facials and creams and puts herself through the expensive ordeal of laser treatments; he has heard all about her adolescent skin traumas.

A full-time environmental activist, Karen has succeeded in saving, for now, the Arizona pygmy owl, but she focuses on her love life, or lack of it. She blames herself, thinks her inability to find love is her fault, for mysterious, possibly karmic reasons. A merchant in a bowler finishes his meal, pays his bill, and tips his hat as he leaves. "God, this Western town thing is so overdone," Karen mutters.

Stefan disagrees. "People need to play-act; they need fantasy." (He imagines gunslingers naked except for their belts and, of course, their holsters and guns.) He pats his lips with a paper napkin. "The meeting was Danny's idea?" He knows the answer: the old high school flame found her on Facebook and made the contact. They exchanged e-mails and photos. Danny is on the chunky side, a large man, is how Karen described him when she forwarded the photos to Stefan, but Stefan thinks he looks like a beer drinker wearing a corset. Of course he didn't say so. This Danny from San Antonio—why a grown heterosexual man would call himself "Danny" is beyond Stefan—was supposed to fly in to spend the weekend, this weekend, with her at the grandly refurbished hotel in Bisbee called The Copper Queen.

Karen shifts in the chair and gives Stefan a patient look. "He said he loves historic hotels. He is passionate about them. He said meeting me at The Copper Queen would be a turn-on."

Stefan knows about The Copper Queen; he once spent three delirious days with a stranger in a corner room.

He snips a brown bit of lettuce from his burger with his fingernails. "Having expectations leads to disappointment, wouldn't you say?" He personally doesn't have expectations, doesn't think about what should or should not be; as a poet, he's long ago decided that his obligation is to observe what is. "You're unrealistic," he adds. She's divorced and forty-five and her looks are on the plain side. Her romantic entanglements usually have shitty endings. She's optimistic and then her hopes are dashed—he used that expression on the drive down from Tucson and she perked up. Told him the archaic expression— "hopes are dashed"—reminded her that the path of love was, indeed, tortuous and fraught. "Tortuous" and "fraught" in the same sentence made the poet in him cringe.

Her countenance is a portrait of disappointment; the lines beside her mouth seem deeper, the circles under her eyes darker. Stefan says, "I didn't mean unrealistic in a negative way."

"Danny was pleased about the idea of meeting in Bisbee. He went to the hotel website and thought it looked super. Then, bango, a message on my cell saying he wasn't coming. One minute he's coming, the next he's not. There's something wrong with me."

He nods sympathetically. What else to do? Karen sets herself up. Any woman who would sign on for ballroom dancing without a partner is asking for rejection. It hadn't turned out badly for either of them. He was the gay man in the class, the sought-after partner—no clammy hands, no clumsy steps— and she, in turn, protected him from overeager widows. They made a good pair; they were light on their feet, anticipated each other's moves, and caught on to new steps quickly. He lives in Phoenix now, two hours north of Tucson. After Danny cancelled, left her high and dry, she phoned him in tears and begged him to come down. She would reimburse him for the twenty-five-minute flight, and because she knows he can't bear sharing a bathroom, she booked him a room for two nights in a nicer motel near her condo. When she picked him up in her white Honda Fit at the airport, they drove east on the I-10 toward Benson. They passed miles and miles of identical housing developments. She said, "Not a solar panel in sight." As soon as she said it, Stefan became conscious of the missing solar panels. Their absence was obvious. Talk about green energy; Tucson has sunshine for more than eighty percent of the year. That's the sort of fact she grabs and runs with.

In Tombstone they went first to the bookstore. Stefan has found his slender volume of poetry in unlikely places, but not here. Not that he actually expected it. The store specializes in the history of the west, with an eye to tourists. They have a few little books of cowboy poems, that's it. He said he was starving, so they went to the café and ordered emu burgers because they sounded exotic.

"What karmic sin did I commit that so many relationships are toast before they begin?" Karen presses her fingers to her eyelids.

The words are so familiar that Stefan says, without thinking, "He has always disappointed you, whatever his name is, he has never given enough." The lines are from a long poem he's written about her but not let her read. He writes about a bitter, older woman too, a character based on her, and though she's read some of the poems, she doesn't realize she's his subject.

"Expectations," he says, getting the conversation back on track.

Karen pushes her plate toward him, crosses her arms on the table, and gives him a steady look. "I suppose I could join *Second Life*."

Stefan flinches. Oh, crap. "Point taken, okay, all right." He'd made the mistake of showing her the online virtual world, *Second Life*, and his avatar, a muscular female bouncer in a lesbian bar. He doesn't date much, so he thought it would be a hoot to hang out with clubbers of the opposite sex. The girls get into such extreme hair-pulling fights, it's hysterically entertaining. Karen deems *Second Life* a waste of time. Get a real life, she tells him, as though hers is working so great.

"Can you get out of it?" He means the hotel booking.

"Nada. Once you make the last confirming click, you kiss your moolah goodbye."

He feels himself relent. "Maybe if you show up in person, they'll take pity on you."

She pays for the lunch at the register and waltzes back to collect her jacket. "You know what? You're right. Let's go. And they have such a great bar."

Stefan blinks, dismayed. That's the other thing about her— she's impulsive. He should have kept his mouth shut.

Bisbee, a half-hour drive south of Tombstone, is situated ten miles north of the Mexican border. He kicks himself as they drive through a landscape of loss (he makes a note on a pad he keeps in his shirt pocket), a settlement of dented trailers, the fronds of one lone palm tree flailing in the wind; a truck with a flat tire, at the driver's window a boy in a red T-shirt glowering; dust devils spinning across the road. She drinks a lot and invariably delivers maudlin monologues, critical of herself and her life. Then she will insinuate, in murmurs, her opinions about him, tiptoeing around the idea that he should get out of his dead-end job in the public records office. Yes, he does gripe, and there's good reason—tedious people surround him. On the other hand, he has a pension to look forward to, and he's not giving it up.

Climbing the wide staircase to the posh hotel, built in the heyday of copper mining when grandees escorted lavishly embellished ladies, Stefan glances at Karen. Because she's blond and has sensitive skin—thin-skinned, she says—her cheeks are red from the wind through the open car window. Before they enter the lobby, she turns to Stefan, places her hand on his arm, her eyes lit. "Just think how incredibly mind-blowing it would have been if Danny was the man I thought he was. It would have been a dream come true."

Stefan winces. From the lobby they turn toward the lounge, the decor plush green velvet, cherry wood, and nickel light fixtures. Believing that dreams come true is another annoying trait of hers. Despite her environmental work and all the losses to developers, she really believes in happy endings, believes the world can be a better place.

They take stools at the black granite bar. She orders a double margarita. Maudlin is on its way. He readies himself for her boozy regrets.

Back in his Phoenix apartment a week later, the sound of the freeway is a depressing, constant whine. His latest batch of poems has been rejected, this time by the publisher of a small press who ostensibly admires his work but can't fit the poems into the existing schedule. It's a blow, when people you trust start stepping sideways. More mail bangs through the slot. He rises from his computer to find a card from her. He opens it eagerly. In the envelope he finds a note and a cheque. The amount is puzzling. It includes the airfare, which he expected, but also a tip for his time. How wonderfully spiteful she is.

Why not cash it? He had hell to go through. All that listening.

The note says, in her angular penmanship:

> I will stay away from you now, knowing you think me exhausting to be around.
>
> I will pick you out of my brain, cell by cell, until you are the stranger you want to be. Giving

you what you want, I relieve you from having a relationship with me.

I banish you.

Stefan is pierced to the heart. She is so arch, so precise when she's angry, and so ruthless, a quality he lacks in his poetry. His poetry tends to lie down, take a meandering view, nothing ball-breaking or cruel or overwrought, as her words are. He reads the note again. Okay, he'd made a few honest observations about her character. The day after Tombstone and The Copper Queen, they'd driven down to Nogales and parked at McDonald's and walked into Mexico, despite the drug wars. Stefan was prattling, nervous. She insisted the restaurant she'd chosen was worth the risk. They'd been seated behind a pillar and she complained until they were reseated, after which the vindictive waiter ignored them. The tortillas were from a package, and the whole day was a bust. His telling her she was demanding was like canned frosting on a crumbling cake.

Traffic is building up; an ambulance, siren sounding delirious, honks and butts its way through. The sky used to be blue, but now the smog is as bad as LA. He places the note and the folded cheque on the table. The cheque is evidence that at last some attention has been paid to his long-suffering friendship.

The ambulance has made it to an off-ramp. He hates this apartment. The building is so shoddily constructed, the walls are so thin, that he can hear the refrigerator door slam in the apartment above his. He wanders over to look into his own fridge. A head of organic cauliflower he paid too much for still looks okay. He'd bought it because he was worried about not consuming enough fibre. She'd phoned to read him a recipe for cauliflower and sweet-potato soup. Chicken broth and something else. Was it coconut milk?

He thinks it was coconut milk. But he'll give her a call. She loves being helpful; she's easily flattered and eager to share. As he reaches for the phone, a thought nags him: She wouldn't really banish him, would she? No, he assures himself, no. She's too loyal. Especially to her suffering.

Coyote Moon

One time—it happened in October, two and a half years ago—
Lee saved a rooster's life. The rooster was a bantam called
Cuthbert, named after an Anglo-Saxon saint. Lee's husband,
Gregory, was into saints and chickens. Cuthbert lived with his
two hens, Irma and Matilda, in a small coop at the bottom of the
unfenced yard, below Lee and Gregory's house in the mountains in the southeast corner of British Columbia. The coop
was situated in the open area before the ground sloped and fell
into a steep ravine that dropped farther to the creek.

In saving Cuthbert's life, Lee didn't do anything daring
like race to rescue him from a pack of dogs, she didn't swat

a vaguely cognizant yearling bear about to go against his fruit-eating nature (that summer had been hot and dry, and huckleberries were scarce), and she didn't shoo the rooster off the road just as a logging truck went rumbling by. Lee's saving of the rooster was quieter and, in its own way, dramatic. Gregory said it was miraculous.

One night, a bear, perhaps desperate with hunger—it was, after all, late in the year and almost time for bears to hibernate—shuffled up from the ravine, sniffed the air and smelled the chickens huddled on their roost, and clawed at the door. Gregory had forgotten to latch it, so the bear shouldered its way inside and broke the roost. It mauled two of the chickens—Irma escaped, as usual—but Matilda and Cuthbert were left wrenched and crumpled on the straw floor. The bear then ate most of the bag of chicken feed and left its signature in the yard: a mound of scat full of plum pits.

In the morning after Lee left for her teaching job at the school, Gregory went down, as he always did, to check on Cuthbert and the girls. He was shocked, he told Lee, to see the old wooden door off its hinges, the scatter of Cuthbert's orange and black feathers, and both tiny, unmoving bodies. He barely glanced in before despair overtook him. He ran around the yard and up onto the road calling for Irma, then turned on his heel and waited in his office at the front of the house for Lee. He was inconsolable, and still teary-eyed when Lee came in the door for lunch.

She marched down the hill to look at the damage and found Cuthbert still throbbing. Matilda was dead, it was true, but poor Cuthbert had existed in a subtle state, hovering between life and death, since the attack. "Gregory," she shouted. "Gregory!" She made him bring a box and fresh straw, lift the rooster, and carry him up to the house. They decided to put the box on top of the freezer, in its own small room with a swinging door. Lying stricken on the straw, Cuthbert looked like a shred of Japanese silk.

When Lee came home from her classroom that afternoon, Gregory seemed calmer; he'd tried giving Cuthbert water through an eyedropper. She moved her hands slowly into the rooster's space until she touched him. She placed her hands side by side on his deflated body. Cuthbert looked at her with one bright little eye. Then he closed it. For ten days, twice a day and sometimes more, she put her hands in the box and let them do the work.

"But did he survive?" This is Sam. He and Lee are sitting in folding chairs in the shade behind the gyro food truck, while Shirley, Sam's wife, finishes cleaning. It's February, and the village south of Tucson, where Lee stays for four months in the winter, is hosting its annual week-long arts and crafts festival. It's her second year of helping out in the gyro truck, and Shirley and Sam have become instant friends, the way people do who are always on the move. From the truck they sell pressed Greek-style minced lamb and beef cooked on a rotating spit, folded into pita bread slathered with tzatziki, shredded lettuce, and cut-up tomatoes. A food truck is a lucrative business, Shirley says. You get your circuit, you stick with it, you show up on time, you're clean, you serve good food. Shirley, a perky blonde from Phoenix with a ponytail and eyes that mean business, is the truck's owner. Her husband, Sam, a younger man on his way to being plump, studied biology at university but short-circuited himself two months shy of his degree. Lee likes him for this; he has a destructive edge.

"Hello? Planet Sam to Planet Lee. Did Cuthbert survive?"

"Of course he survived. Didn't I say that Gregory used the word 'miraculous'? Would I have said 'miracle' if Cuthbert had died?" Sam has heard about Gregory's death but hasn't heard Cuthbert's full story, far more graphic: After the first day he struggled to his feet, his neck so bent his comb touched the bottom of the box, and stood for a moment before sinking like a balloon leaking air. A thick, bloody mucous hung from his beak. "His neck is broken," Gregory had said. "No, it is not," she'd said, sounding annoyed. They took turns feeding him a soupy gruel of ground chicken mash and water. "He's going to die," Gregory had said. "No, he's not," she'd said, adamant. Cuthbert came to recognize her voice as she soothed him, and he blinked as though sending her messages from afar. After eight days, he lifted his head a little and took a halting step. Two days later he raised his head above the top of the box.

"He survived," she says again to Sam.

It's warm and sunny—she wears cotton pants and a pair of running shoes—but in the days before the festival, vendors just arriving worried that a rainy streak wouldn't let up. Now everything is so thirsty you'd never know weather had been a concern. Lee smells the heat and dust and dryness. Her skin is always crying for cream or sunscreen in this climate; her hands are parched, the backs patchy with spreading freckles and whitish spots she'd rather not think about. People stroll by, talking and laughing, stuffing food into their mouths, mariachi music in the background from the Mexican restaurant in another lane. The festival draws huge crowds and takes place in a village two thousand miles south of the village where Lee saved Cuthbert and where Gregory, she believes, despite what others say, killed himself.

"What happened to Irma?" Sam wants to know. He has big brown eyes and unruly hair.

"What are you saying?" Lee thinks about the astonishment on Gregory's face the day that Cuthbert wobbled to his feet and stayed there. Gregory had been diligent in feeding Cuthbert mash and water with a baby spoon and eyedropper, yet repeatedly he told Lee she was wasting her time. The day Cuthbert stood up, Gregory smelled of quinine and bergamot and he'd been wearing the same shirt for three days; he hadn't won the contract he expected, after all. And soon after that, as though (she'd thought at the time) the blow to his career was the last straw, he took a noticeable number of pills, a combination of Aspirin, Tylenol, and maybe a dozen Benadryl, the drugs that she'd assumed killed him. The autopsy uncovered the fact that he had kidney cancer, advanced and undiagnosed. His death wasn't ruled a suicide. He would have been in great pain. Why hadn't he told her? Why had she been so oblivious?

The trumpet in the mariachi band blares its solo.

"You said Irma escaped."

"Oh, Irma." Gregory's death remains sad and confusing; Lee just can't figure why she didn't have some wifely insight that he was so ill. "Irma escaped from that bear twice," she says. Irma was such a survivor that when the bear came again, the chicken ran to the house and threw herself against the sliding glass door, just as the ambulance was on its way for Gregory. Lee, distracted when she spotted Irma frantic against the glass, had slid the door open to let her in and then forgot about her. Irma pooped all over the living room before hunkering down beside a basket of straw flowers. Only a serene clucking led Lee to her the next day, after Gregory was pronounced dead and the whole spinning house came to a stop.

"Christ, *Irma* was saved. Why not Gregory?" Had she noticed anything wrong, anything that stood out? No, she had not.

"We don't get choices," Sam says. "What about Cuthbert?"

"What?"

"What about Cuthbert when the bear came back?"

"Oh, he ran into the bush and came out when I called him.

He knew me. He seemed so grateful to see me, it made me cry." Cuthbert had followed Lee back to the chicken coop, repaired by a neighbour. Irma was already inside, so Cuthbert was happy. "So there they are, Cuthbert and Irma, and here I am, Lee alone."

Shirley steps down from the truck, mop in hand. It's not that she likes to do everything related to sanitation and hygiene, but she does it because Sam is so bad at it. "It was fate," she says to Lee. She takes the band out of her ponytail and shakes her hair.

Shirley won't use the word *death* or *dying* or *dead*, so Lee says, "What was fate?"

"That Gregory moved on." She taps her toe against the front tire of Lee's new Schwinn cruiser that leans against the trunk of a mesquite tree.

"Yeah, moved on," Lee says. She likes them because they don't mind listening to her theories about what happened to Gregory. They don't think she should have "moved on" from her loss. She stands, stretches her back. "See you later."

She dingles the bell on the handlebar and rides away past the food stalls—the Indian fry bread and taco trucks, the pizza stand with red-and-white striped umbrellas out front, the corn-dog and cotton candy trucks—and turns onto the lane where she rents the apartment above a fine arts gallery. Her landlord, Derek, and his partner play opera in the mornings while they dust and tidy, open boxes that arrived in yesterday's delivery, and set the new paintings and ceramics in place before opening the store. Passionate arias wake her every morning, and she lies in bed listening, Mr. PurrBunny asleep at her feet, realizing she is far from home, and this realization causes feelings both satisfied and unsettling.

From her canvas chair on the gallery's flat roof that serves as a deck, Lee has long views, over the freeway and, in the distance, the rocky orange mountains to the west, as well as the make-shift campground in the bare yard below where three vendors stay. She hears the sizzle of burgers on a portable grill. Shirley says Derek lets these particular long-time vendors set up their booths in front of his store, and camp out back, because Derek's store doesn't sell photographs of the Grand Canyon or beaded jewellery boxes or antique postcards. ("Cynical," Sam says of Shirley.) The vendors—one of them a Bavarian photographer who wears a green alpine hat with a feather—live in vans or tent trailers and pull small U-Hauls for their wares. They're set up adjacent to the ravine, called a wash, a natural catchment for rain during Arizona's monsoons in July and August. Across the wash, she can see lights from a restaurant, the bookstore, and other galleries. A male Gambel's quail calls his harem with a cry that sounds like *Chi-cago, Chi-cago.* From her vantage point Lee watches the Bavarian photographer throw something to his yippy little dog. She remembers this dog from last year.

She hears the squeak of the door downstairs. Derek appears from under the line of the roof and, limping slightly, moseys over to the campers. Cooking meat this late in the evening will bring the coyotes closer, she knows he'll tell them. Last week a coyote killed the restaurant cat; the screeches were terrible. She didn't mind that the cat was dead; it was an aggressive black male that would climb the stairs, jump onto the balcony, and hiss through the window at her own Mr. PurrBunny.

A month or so ago, Lee hurried into the kitchen to make a quick sandwich and saw a huge rat, the size of a squirrel, panting in a corner. When she shrieked, Mr. PurrBunny leapt to the counter and from there to the top of the fridge, where he, the coward, watched Lee scramble around, find her gum boots, plaid jacket, and fur-lined gloves in order to corral the thing and not get bitten. Wearing those items from home, her Canadian clothes she calls them, made her feel brave. She herded the rat into the spare room that stored boxes she would repack when she left and shut the door. She used a strategy of boxes laid side by side six inches from the wall to create an alley. The box at the end, long enough to hold a table lamp, was open. Using a broom, she herded the rat along the makeshift passageway. Once he scooted into the box, she screwed up her courage, flipped it upright. She heard him scrabbling around in the bottom. She taped the top shut with duct tape. Muttering curses, she dragged it downstairs and knocked on the gallery's back door. Derek answered. Behind him she could see the supplies in the mailroom. "I found a rat in the apartment," she said. She set the box down on its side and waited to see his reaction.

"Is it in there?" Derek pointed and Lee nodded. He stepped out from the doorway and stomped on the middle. The box moved, kind of rocked, scuffling on the gravel. Derek stepped hard again and dented another section. They could see where the rat made a bulge. Derek took aim, brought his heavy shoe down a third time, and the bulge flattened out. Lee felt a stir of admiration; she hadn't known Derek harboured such anger, such merciless violence just waiting to erupt; it was impossible to guess the depths of another's pent-up rage.

When she came back upstairs, Mr. PurrBunny was busy sniffing the trail of the rat through the apartment, from the cat door through the kitchen and into the spare room. He gave her an accusing look. She sat down at her computer and realized who the culprit was. Mr. PurrBunny. He had brought in the rat. Somehow he'd held that gigantic rat in his jaws all the way up the stairs, across the balcony, and through the cat door. She wondered if she'd known it was Mr. PurrBunny when she accused Derek of having rats in the building; she thinks perhaps she had. What was wrong with her? Why had she been so insensitive? "What a cat," she said, by way of making him, and herself, feel better, and stroked him, but Mr. PurrBunny didn't raise his head from his pillow. She cocked an eyebrow. "Are you holding a grudge?"

No answer.

When she'd told Sam about the incident, he said, "Didn't you feel bad for the rat?"

"You must be kidding. It was a *rat*."

"But that was cruel, the way Derek killed it."

"I'm not responsible for what Derek did," Lee said, suddenly lost, suddenly thinking, *Gregory. What Gregory did.* She slapped her hands together.

Sam blinked, startled. "You will never be a Buddhist."

"The rat was in my territory. I'm a coyote. Think of me that way."

"Coyote is more than Trickster. Coyote means adaptability. Wisdom."

"Bullshit," Lee said.

Shortly after Gregory died, a colleague, someone almost a friend, invited her to lunch.

The friend told Lee how amazing she was: "You're on your feet, walking and talking, doing so well."

This particular restaurant, owned by gay men, was in a nearby town and was known for its fresh, local ingredients. On the small table by the window where they sat, a crystal vase held a single iris. Lee studied the iris, the tight folds of mauve and cream, hints of its future glory. She wore Gregory's wedding ring on her left thumb, holding on to it for him; she didn't yet believe he was dead for good. She was in the philosophical stage of grief, a confident period of waiting for fate to change its mind. She and Gregory had been married for nine years. After all, Cuthbert and Irma were back together after surviving their ordeals with the bear. Anything was possible.

The friend said, "My worst nightmare is my husband dying."

The friend said, "I wouldn't be able to function like you are; *I* would have to be scraped off the floor or the walls."

The friend said, "I envy you your freedom."

Lee had looked up then.

Shirley and Sam are over, to drink wine on Lee's second little balcony, the one that faces the street. Lee tells them the story of the lunch but can't recall whether it was the floor or the walls that her friend said she would have to be scraped from. "Scraped, anyway," she says, handing Sam the second bottle to open. His hands are warm, and he has a sweet smile. "She envied me my freedom."

"Coyotes don't whinge or whine," Sam says.

"Jesus." Shirley wears a calculated, disgusted look. "That was so shitty of her."

"I didn't think so at first. Now I do."

"Coyotes get on with things."

"What is this shit about you and coyotes?" Shirley asks Sam and sits up in her chair.

"Hey, hey," he says, and she settles back.

The friend had talked about her own second marriage, the difficult children, her dependence on the man. If he died, she would too.

Lee had told her, "No, you wouldn't." Then changed the subject.

She takes Shirley's empty glass.

"What a bitch," says Shirley.

"This earth is purgatory, that's my theory," Sam says and pours another round. They clink glasses, Lee's new ones from Cost Plus.

"See, that's why I love him," Shirley says. "Thoughts like that never enter my head. I live in the moment, count money, move on."

"That's why I married you. To follow orders."

Then their banter: "Oh, yeah?" "Make something of it, why don't you," as they drink up and prepare to leave.

She sits on the balcony, the glasses dried and put away. People are still wandering the streets, though the vendors have closed their booths and stored their wares in locked vans. She hears a radio, some laughter, smells smoke from a bonfire from another camp. In the distance, the quail call each other home; the coyotes lead off with some preliminary yipping. They stop; they will break up, separate, slink around in the moonlight.

She hears someone on the outside stairs and turns to the screen door. The Bavarian photographer holds his feathered hat in his hand. He says, "Excuse me. Have you seen our dog? The little white one?"

"Oh." Lee takes a moment.

"Buddy's adventurous. He has no idea he's so small."

"Buddy?"

"Our dog. The wife's dog."

She hears the yip of a coyote. "Oh, that sweetie," says Lee. She can't clearly see the man waiting in the dark, but she knows the expression on his face: despair around the mouth. She looks at her hands. These hands helped to wreck a rat's life. These hands saved the life of a rooster, but not the life of a man. She glances back in the direction of the door. Hope may be better than no hope. "I saw him a little earlier, heading to the food court." This may be the kindest thing she's said in weeks.

Coyotes yelp in celebration of a kill, so when the real ruckus begins and fills the night with bloody festivity, Lee's heart lifts too. What is the wisdom in loss? What is she supposed to learn? For now, she wants something chased down; she, too, carries grudges. The stars rise like diamonds from behind the mountains into the vivid sky, deep indigo and mauve. This is the first truly dark place Lee has ever lived; nightly she experiences miracles.

Borderline

You burp, it's rancid, you lie in your crib wet and hungry, a strip of light coming through a partially open door separating you from her. You mutter, the pit of your stomach burns then cramps, your legs fly up and squirts eject, and there you are, in your crib wet, hungry, and now smelly. You mutter some more, you try *ba-ba-ba-ba*. You stare at the strip of light through which she will pass. She doesn't come. You wave your arms, wanting the smell of her, the taste of her skin around her jaw and chin that you try to mouth. Your flower-stalk head waits for the weight of her hand to hold it up. Glimpsing her you're all astir, aflutter, in a quiver of expectation. Slam. Click. Light gone.

God. When I told this story to my first psychiatrist, back in Toronto, he said there was no way I could remember. Ridiculous. I remember lying stunned and staring into the pitch-black. No hands, no fingers, no legs, no body, no mind. I remember being an invisible baby, flailing useless arms, blinking in darkness, panic rising. "When I stopped my stupid whimpering and crying, I wasn't sure if I was still alive," I told him.

"Ah, but you have to learn to wait your turn. You are one among many. The ego," he said.

By then a grown woman with choices, my ego mobilized and stretched itself large. "Me, me, me, me, me, me, me!" I shrieked, startling us both. I stamped to the door, passed through, let it slam shut. A few steps into the waiting room, I heard a sound, a clicking sound, and turned back, tried the handle. He had locked the door from the inside. I could hear his muffled voice on the phone.

I almost passed out—that was dangerous.

I've learned there's waiting. Of course there's waiting. There's always waiting. Wintering between two American border checkpoints—one, to the south, at the actual border to Mexico, and the other just twenty-five miles north, on the northbound lanes of the I-19 freeway inside the state of Arizona—you learn about waiting. Twice a week I drive to Tucson for appointments with my psychiatrist and I have learned to allow extra time at the checkpoint—you must wait your turn. The Border Patrol calls the permanent roof over the I-19 a "canopy," but to me, and some others, the eight-hundred-and-seventy-thousand-dollar structure looks like the military installation it is, the Quonset hut roof embedded with spotlights.

I slow and turn up the car radio to hear the news on NPR, to hear English. The radio in my apartment, its antenna pointing hopefully northward, catches only static or staccato Spanish. The second-hand TV is useless too; occasionally I glimpse Oprah behind the snow. I can't sign a cable agreement; they want a year commitment. A snowbird, I'm just in Arizona for five months.

Yes, here comes the flying roof. Border Patrol is siphoning traffic into one lane using orange dunce hat cones. Along with white trucks full of produce on ice, or cars crowded with Mexican families up for the day, or maybe someone like me, working on something that won't ever be clear, I fall into a resigned line. Everyone wants to avoid the "secondary inspection," where they pull you over into a special holding area and strip your vehicle. According to the law, they don't have to have real suspicion; they can "select" you for a conversation, and, in my case, I don't trust what might come out of my mouth. The goal is not to say anything provocative or to annoy them; I tell myself that deeply, truly I do not want to be noticed.

The sniffing dog worries the white van five vehicles ahead, the German shepherd at attention on a leash held by a guy twice as big as my small-boned son, a computer nerd locked in a university lab in Toronto. The dog's nose ciphers a vehicle's life over the years. What kind of stories would a piece of steel with tires reveal? How would anybody explain: I was young then. Hey, I have no bombs.

So now to prepare: Turn the volume on the radio down to zero (NPR is considered "left wing"), tidy the front seat, smooth an eyebrow with a pinkie, and open the window. A glance in the mirror informs me that my eyes are red from the mesquite pollen, so in go allergy drops to take the red out. Inching forward, I smile but not too much, turn off the phone, and seem preoccupied with the shopping list beside me, too preoccupied to look them in the eye. Here's how it is, as I see it: You slide on by. Wade your way through the checkpoint like Mexicans crossing a river. Practise looking guiltless: a gift of the state.

They wave me on. They hardly look at me.

Surging through the guilt gate once again, I turn up the volume. The news makes my spirits rise—nutcases act out all over the world. I pass the Tohono O'odham reservation with its mystical white church off in the distance and dive into Tucson traffic.

Personality disorders—borderline or narcissistic—make you erratic, unreliable in general. My analyst—the Tucson shrink—says, "You have to catch yourself in the act. You have to stop shouting and hear yourself."

"But why am I like this?"

"Work with what you have," he says.

The state of my mind is attributed to genetics, familial tendencies. Upbringing. There is that locked-up uncle. But at forty-nine, I've realized others aren't the ones I should be suspicious of, it's me.

"You seem sad."

The analyst opens with his usual gambit. By the time I arrive, park behind the little square building, climb the stairs—those extra ten pounds—and enter his office with its fake leather couch and the twist of modern glass trying to look vaguely phallic, I do feel sad. "I hate the Border Patrol. They piss me off. I hate having to be nice because I'm afraid." I've stepped into it now.

"What happens if you're not nice?"

"They'll arrest me. They won't like me. They don't anyway. They hardly noticed me." I pause, then blurt: "I'll be in an insane asylum or be dead, the kid alone on the playground. Scabby knees. Dirty arms. Damn." He picks up on "dirty arms." Feeling childish and defensive now, I say, "I used to show up at Sunday school with dirty arms. When I put my elbows on the table, the undersides of my arms were streaky with dirt. I had to hide them from my Sunday school teacher. She would notice."

If he were permitted to smile, he would, I can feel it. But he doesn't smile. I watch him as closely as a baby watches its mother's mouth. Sometimes because of the watching, I can't understand a word.

He says, "How did you feel?"

"I would turn bright red."

"Embarrassed?"

"Humiliated. Could never remember to wash my arms. I tried, and there they'd be, dirty."

"Whose job do you think it was to see you were clean before Sunday school?"

"Mine. I was old enough. I just missed my arms."

"It was your fault?"

"I never told my mother."

"But she should have noticed."

"I wasn't worth noticing." Bang. Click.

Silence. He gives me a moment. Tears are on the way. I won't give them to him. I won't give in. But he's paid not to quit.

"What makes you think you weren't worth noticing?"

It's all I can do to stay in this room, all I can do to not stand, walk to the door, and shut it behind me—oh so quietly. I'll be like a waft of air, a mere breeze passing through, a moment he won't remember.

He says quietly, "How do you feel now?"

What I feel is nothing. Dead nothingness, the centre of me as empty as a void, shreds of pride clinging to my skull. But another emotion awakens; I know this one, a form of excess that in my experience can only make matters worse. Righteousness. Righteousness rouses, vaults out from its dark place to fill the gap, to lift me up—I have good reasons to hate this man, to hate myself. I'll swallow the pills I hoard, I'll rip up the cheque I've written and mail him the pieces. I'll eat a whole movie-theatre-sized box of Junior Mints. *Junior Mints.* My laugh sputters out there, sounds like someone choking.

"Paula, what's going on, on the inside?"

I won't tell him. Won't say a word. My head roars. Blank space. Then: It's rude not to say something. "None of your fucking goddamn business."

Silence.

Mental static amid heartbeats.

He waits, gaze level, practised, attentive. It's hard to catch him blinking. I take a breath. I *am* making progress—I am noticing his look. "I hate you."

"I know."

The kindness in his voice is like a thrust with a weapon, it hurts that much. The pain enters my pelvis first, moves up my spine, and brings tears to my eyes.

"It's hard for you when someone's nice," he says. "How do you feel?"

He's working me, slowly dragging me back. "Borderline personality disorder, remember?" I've read the American Psychiatric Association's DSM description.

"I don't believe in labels."

"I do." It was shocking to see my "unique" selfhood described so accurately.

"Labels are limiting."

"Definitions are useful." Behaviours that I thought my own

turn out to be based on a personality disorder. It's so fucking ironic that my life is hassled with border checkpoints.

"It's hard for you to be vulnerable." He smiles a genuine, likeable smile. Sometimes I attempt to entertain him, to elicit that smile. "When we've been ignored by our mother and someone notices us, we overreact."

To stand back and see yourself as others see you—a person whose conduct is predictable, based on brain chemistry—makes you feel like a specimen, a lesser human. All those years I thought I was thinking. No. Just acting out.

Silence.

Then he skips a few lines. "When someone is kind, do you feel an inner excitement?"

He has me, and I can't help it—I scoot forward. "Yes! I start bubbling and want to move in."

"Move in?"

"If someone is nice, I just want to move in, have them all to myself, attach myself like a barnacle." My body prickles with a sense of urgency; I've confessed a deeply tangled truth that gives rise to helplessness and panic. I must disengage immediately. I pick an object to stare at. The twist of coloured glass he thinks is art. There, that choice is unsurprising, conventional. Boring, just like him. What does he know? What does he really know? My eyes slide sideways toward his. The bottom line is, I want him to love me.

He says it gently as he stands: "Our time is up."

"Thank God." As always, I try for more attention. We've talked about it. I say, "You can't wait to get rid of me."

Driving southbound, at first I'm dazed and practically deaf, my mind cycling through the mixed signals: what I said, what he said. What I shouldn't have said, the disgrace and unbearable discomfort of wanting so much. As anger rises, I deliberately turn my attention to the checkpoint, to the long, sullen line of vehicles at a standstill, then begin to gloat, an unsettling feeling that's nevertheless better than the first one. Then fury leaps to the fore, despising me, the fury a predator that operates most successfully in the hell of psychic confusion. The next thing I know, I'm cursing a blue streak and *Why the hell, How the hell* is the mild part of it. My swearing accelerates to shouting, then I'm screaming, foot pressing the pedal, the car picking up speed. Then I yell, "Stop! Stop shouting, stop shouting!" I want to bulldoze the falling-apart Pontiac in front of me, a mattress strapped to the roof. I shout, "Stop!" again. Someone looks at me from another car and I glimpse myself in the mirror, see in a flash that I'm off track. I have to get off the freeway, pull the car over, bring myself to a halt. The next exit is a long way yet. I grit my teeth, scream through them, swing onto an exit ramp, slow at the bottom. The tendons in my neck hurt from bellowing.

I pull into a Walmart parking lot and drive over to an empty section. I leave the engine on and the radio up—to hell with NPR, I want loud, violent music—rap!—to muffle the conversation zapping back and forth between me and myself, accusations flying because everyone ignored me, I can't stand being ignored, I'm angry for being so stupid, so pitiful, so wrong. I shouldn't have been born, everything about me is stupid, everyone hates me, I hate myself, they didn't even look at me at the checkpoint, they didn't think I was worth looking at, the shrink dismisses me, how can you do this, how can you do this to yourself. If I had a gun, I would fire it.

My hands on the steering wheel hold me in place as my body goes through the raging. The holding is exhausting, an act of will, because mentally I want to give in, everything I feel about the world and myself in it is true and yet, and yet I know it's not the only truth. I am not only my personality disorder and I break into a sweat with the effort of holding on to that thought. My hands hurt—fucking hands, fuck that!

A police officer taps on the window. My startle reflex working overtime, I cry out and fumble to start the car, but it's already on, isn't it, and the air conditioning is blasting and the rap station is pounding and so is my head. I turn the radio off and slide both front windows down. "Oh, dear." I dab at my eyes, then gesture toward the phone on the seat. "I've had some bad news." I see myself in his Polaroid cop glasses—my hair's a mess, I've scratched my face, my eyes look crazy. "But I'll be fine."

He leans in the passenger side window, inhales, sniffing.

They have their priorities, I think, and with this thought I begin to calm down, flutter my fingers to seem that I'm tidying my hair. The officer asks, "May I see your registration?" I open the glove compartment. He looks at the documents, nods, hands my papers back. "Nice time of year for you snowbirds." I assure him, yes it is. He lifts his hands off the sill and, changing his mind, looks in again. "You have someone at home to check on you?" I reply that I do indeed. My son, a good boy. He lives here. "We all get bad news one time or another. You drive slow and take care now, ma'am." And simple as that he turns and walks away. I watch the patrol car swing out onto the road and am so relieved that at last I feel the pounding of my heart. My God, what was I thinking, what was I doing?

Walking across the parking lot, I pay attention to the physical sensations, to my breathing, to the right toe with the bunion that hurts, the warm tarmac on the soles of my shoes, the olive trees emitting pollen that make my eyes itch more, the screeching great-tailed grackles, black birds with long tails and yellow eyes. Entering Walmart, I ignore the carts and the Mac-sized people pushing them, and head straight to the back where there's a washroom. In front of a mirror, I know the drill—comb my hair, pat down my face with a wet paper towel, apply allergy eye drops, blow my nose, smooth on a new coat of foundation to hide the scratch, paint my lips with lipstick, tap a finger to my lips, and add some colour to my cheeks. There.

I walk back through the store, attentive to the children running, the stacks of DVDs on sale, the music in the background, the smell of hot dogs and popcorn, the piles of boxes filled with chemicals disguised as food.

Outside, I make my way through the multicoloured array of cars, then drive to a nearby carwash and sit inside as machines shoot water and soap, and spinning rollers lather my vehicle. I have time to think. The moods are quick as a tornado no one has sighted. They come without a physical warning, unlike, so I understand, an epileptic seizure, where a person might have a subtle intimation. What caused this uproar? A border guard not noticing me? I must be crazy. Please, God, let me be ignored. And thank God for the police officer who walked away.

The car jerks forward to the vacuum dry. The light is red. Agitation subsides, sinks back to wherever it lives. As hoses blast the car with air, I shudder. I think, *Work with what you have.*

The light turns green.

Managing to hum a little in the quiet after the storm, I park behind my building. A man about my age who rents an apartment near mine—I've seen him walking a border collie—stops to talk. "Listen, I gather you go to Tucson a lot."

My antennae go up. I cover with a lame rejoinder. "You've got a border collie. Does that you mean you work for the Border Patrol?" I can't prevent this sort of comment, but he laughs.

"We know everything about you, what can I say? I've signed the petitions against the damn thing, but I'm afraid it won't go away."

"I signed 'Citizens for Freedom' with a fake name, and I'm not even a citizen."

"Noble of you," he says, smiling. "The Kinsmen are having a shoe giveaway this weekend and we need people to pick up shoes—good ones, really expensive dressy ones—in Tucson. Would you be willing?"

I cross my arms. "Dressy? I haven't heard the word *dressy* in years." Damn. Not nice. I uncross my arms. "Who are the shoes for, cocktail waitresses?"

The border collie lunges at the leash. The man frowns and takes a step away.

"Wait! Listen. Yes, I will. Pick up shoes. Any kind, I don't care. I'm Paula."

"I know." He pulls the dog up. "As I said, we know everything about you." He raises an eyebrow, waits, and then, smiling, relents. "The gallery. I've seen you at the art gallery. I'm Robert, a volunteer there. You once said we had better stationery than the museum in Tucson." The dog sits, eyes me as though I might need herding.

I may, indeed, need herding.

Robert explains that the shoe giveaway is for the working poor. Yard maintenance men, motel housekeepers, caregivers to the elderly, people earning minimum wage, people who live in sneakers from Walmart, where many of them work. "The surprising thing we do is turn the situation on its ear. We give away really expensive shoes, the leftovers from high-end stores. And our customers enjoy what we're doing and so they're very particular. We measure shoe size because people often don't know what size they are. You should see the pleasure on a hospital cleaner's face when she's wearing a perfectly fitted, beautiful shoe."

I listen and like the idea that the recipients will be picky about styles and sizes. Certainly I like turning a situation on its ear. Robert suggests that I consider volunteering. "People will be lined up hours in advance, and it's pandemonium once the door opens."

I nod. "I understand pandemonium."

"We've done the big-batch pickup but some better, smaller mall stores are coming in on it, so it's a boon. Thanks." He salutes and turns to walk away. "I'll be in touch."

I blink. The light is so bright it buzzes. The buzzing becomes excitement, coursing through my body. I watch him and the dog until they round the corner.

In the apartment, I head to the bathroom mirror and look at my watch. I will stand for five minutes until the excitement passes. He saw me; he talked to me. My fingers touch my face. Yes, this soft skin is mine, the wrinkle between the eyes mine. The dark eyebrows that arch a bit too much as though surprised, those are mine too. I reach in my makeup drawer and add eyeliner, then fill in the brows with eyebrow pencil and step back. There—almost—is a reasonably calm face. Don't study the eyes, just glance. I check my watch. One minute to go.

When time's up, I fiddle tuning the radio, listen to the pops, snaps, and static, look longingly at the door and consider grabbing a sunhat and running after Robert. I'll offer to make dinner, I'll help him walk the dog, I'll nestle right up to him, *move in*. I hear myself say, *I just want to move in* to the shrink. A lively Mexican pop song breaks through, a surprise. I look at the radio thoughtfully, glance again at the door. Tell myself no. I will collect footwear and then measure and fit tired feet. Just that. I kick my own shoes off, step to the kitchen sink, and turn the water on full blast. Drink one glass and then another for the sake of something to do, for the feeling of fullness.

Desert Dreams

Nina stops at a Walgreen's on Speedway to buy a bottle of shiraz, and then stands outside in the sun to phone her mother. She can see a Taco Bell on the corner. "How about crispy tacos?" Miriam loves crispy tacos. It's Thursday night, and on Thursdays Nina arranges dinner for the two of them in Miriam's suite. Miriam says, "Just the ticket." Her retirement complex doesn't serve Mexican or Chinese food, Miriam's favourites. Sometimes Nina cooks in the suite's efficiency kitchen. Her pancakes and eggs-over-easy are a hit; Miriam loves real maple syrup and Trader Joe's cage-free eggs and brags about them as though she's been using them for the last fifty years so that the "chickens have a free life, like us."

When Miriam employs irony with the captives in the wheel-chair exercise class, sometimes Nina knows because someone on staff informs her. "Folks don't like to be reminded of their situation, and your mother's jokes . . ."

"People don't know how to laugh," Miriam says, wiping her face with a dishtowel (crunchy taco bits are everywhere), when Nina broaches the topic. "What's the matter with those dumb birds . . . can't see the forest for the trees."

Nina interprets her mother's occasionally slurred speech—a result of Parkinson's—and her "forest for the trees" remark as meaning elderly people who are ill aren't free and you might as well laugh about it. "Is that what you mean?"

Miriam gives her a look with a shrewd blue eye. "Close," she says. Nina nabs a shred of lettuce from Miriam's cheek, taco pieces from her mother's bib and the cushion, then drops to her knees to pick pieces from the rug and from around the carved lions' feet of her mother's chair.

"Silvie is coming in the morning," Miriam says, waving a hand, which means don't bother. But Silvie hasn't cleaned since the house in Portland. Miriam wrinkles her nose. "Do I smell gasoline?"

"Yes." Nina explains the fiasco she had earlier with a gas nozzle, how it got away.

"First funny thing I've heard all day," Miriam says, her consonants sounding clear, and then she laughs behind her hand to hide her mirth.

Walking back from the RV park laundry room under the eerie sulphur-coloured streetlights obliterating the desert stars, Nina doesn't follow the cement paths. Since Frank's death she forces herself to act brave, and so she walks in sandals and defies a scorpion to sting her. Her little camper is parked ahead, its porch light on, steadfast as it waits for her in a row with others, bigger units, shinier rigs, owned by couples. When she explains her mother's situation, they commiserate and pat her arm—all safe as houses in this gated, winter community. She misses Oregon, the green ruggedness of Oregon. She misses the mists and rain, the palette of cool, clean colours, the restless ocean. After Frank died, she drove to the coast, to practise towing the sixteen-foot travel trailer behind the blue Explorer he'd bought them, stayed overnight in motels or RV parks to keep herself out of the house, away from their bed, away from his "King of Hearts" coffee mug. She'd sketched breakers surging against offshore rocks, pounding on them, white foam spewing.

Her plan is to take Miriam back home with her, but Miriam won't go. Miriam hates the desert; she came for the winter sun and then, according to her, she met a bunch of idiots, and now is caught in the same net. Whatever that means.

Nina finishes the wine. At 1:00 AM she lies awake, gazing at a slice of moon. A country singer warbles, "Sometimes you're the windshield, sometimes you're the bug."

Miriam is rooting for her, hoping, Nina suspects, that on the road she will stumble onto the perfect companion, and that the new man will stop her from moping. "Mope, mope," Miriam says. "Hanging out with old people, get out of that place," she says about the compound where Nina's staying. "I don't need you," Miriam insists. "Go get a life."

"Why aren't you worried about me travelling alone?"

"Why should I worry? You're no spring chicken, doll face." Then Miriam tells her to buy some decent clothes, hit Vegas. She uses the world *flirt* or maybe *lurk*. Lurking around Vegas, just the ticket.

Here it is, the end of March and the end of spring in the scrap desert between the Mohave and the bright lights of Vegas, and Nina has driven and camped for two weeks, working in water-colour, painting flowers that survive despite the arid, often bleak and inhospitable landscape. The project has provided her with a purpose. The burden of being followed everywhere by her own home is an inescapable preoccupation too; for long moments she hurts less about Frank. Last night, camped at a truck stop in Blythe, she was making ordinary love to him with all the loving kisses she gave him when he was alive. The spirit of him was in her but no silky penis; she didn't have an orgasm. Then in the dream she was washing towels, green and blue. There had been the dream, the hot wind, stars twinkling through the tiny window, her aching hip.

She's driven through Needles, a Route 66 town on the border between California and Arizona, and once again can't find a campground. She'll dry-camp again—no water hook-up, no electricity, but she has water aboard and propane for cooking and running the refrigerator—and turns in to park behind a gas station. But when she takes a quick look around, she spots a dark truck and the light of a cigarette in the cab. She turns the ignition over and moves on, cruising slowly along the highway, searching for a safer place—not too isolated, no garbage strewn about, no single wide trailer surrounded by wrecked cars and rusted appliances.

In a pull-out on her right, a white Chevy Silverado towing a Prowler camper trailer is tucked near some eucalyptus trees. The Silverado, nosed toward the road, has left room for an escape. If you pin yourself in a tight spot with the bad guys coming, you're open to ambush; Westerns taught her that. She circles back to the Silverado, slides by slowly to take another look at it and the Prowler. The vehicle is newish and in good condition. Michelin tires, good tread. Though the Prowler isn't a new model, what counts are the blinds. Blinds that are dented or askew are a sure sign of a mean dog or a single man falling apart.

The blinds of the Prowler are orderly.

She lowers her windows so that anyone watching can see that she's by herself. Her theory is that a man with a gun will holster it if he sees a woman of her age travelling alone, and if he's a good man, he'll feel protective. The best place to park, Frank had said, is slightly behind the other rig so you're visible through the driver's side rear-view but not situated so that someone sitting outside will feel spied on.

She sits in the sweltering cab and waits for her intuition to catch up.

Fine.

She settles in.

A man from the Prowler, wearing a straw hat, catches her dumping a pot of hot water used for cooking penne pasta into the ditch. He introduces himself as Louis Shaw and tips the hat. His hair is wavy, grey, a good cut. His plaid shirt is spotless, his nails clean. He's Frank's size, a size she likes, solid, not sinewy.

She lets Louis Shaw see her looking at him.

He says he's travelling with his son, a young man recently divorced. They're on a father–son bonding trip. She raises her hand to her eyes, looks toward the Prowler.

"You won't see him," Louis Shaw says. "He's depressed." She's glimpsed a figure, ducking in and out with something in his arms. "We have a cat," the man says, following her eyes, a man who has an answer for everything. She wonders, nonchalantly, if they're nuts—the skulking son, the blunt man, the cat. Probably feral, the three of them.

A cactus wren, a confident bird with a distinctive eye

stripe, stalks out from under the brush to check the tire treads for treats. It disappears under her Explorer. Louis Shaw says, "Arizona state bird." He looks down at his feet. Nina watches him, curious. He murmurs, apologetically, "I want to make love to you."

At first she wonders if she's heard right. She peers at him as he raises his head. His eyes are hazel. Dark freckles spread across his cheeks, the skin fine against the hard bone. The expression on his face is pleasant. She waits to see how she feels. Not panicky. Not anxious. Not afraid. She says, "You would, would you?"

Her comment brings a shy nod, some twitching in the hands.

"That's lovely." She touches her cheek, looks sideways at him. "I have a bottle of wine. Would you care to sit down? You'll have to bring your own chair." Inside the camper, she locks the door as a precaution, and slips the pasta out of the strainer into a bowl, tosses it with olive oil, puts a plate over it. The wine is already chilled; there is nothing as reliable as a Dometic-brand three-way fridge. She fluffs her short hair in the mirror over the sink.

She climbs onto the bed, reaches into the elongated storage space above it for the wineglasses, and unwraps them from their protective towels.

"It's only a cheap shiraz," she says, outside again. The camper shields them from the highway, but she's heard a string of fast cars go by. Dust floats in the hot air and settles slowly.

"Red," she adds. Some people don't know a white grape from a red one. He's brought a typical aluminum folding chair. Green stripes.

"Oh, I know." He looks at the label. "The Australians are oaky. But the wines are predictable and generally inexpensive. A good bargain."

She smiles, offers him the expensive corkscrew.

He places the bottle on her step. "I see. You're a connoisseur." The cork eases out with a subdued pop. "I shouldn't drink."

So he's an alcoholic. Perhaps there's a weakness in him that his son has to look after.

"It's Lent. I was giving up wine for Lent."

"Oh." That information makes her mind reel in another direction—religion, responsibilities, respectability. "You should have told me. I wouldn't have served you wine."

"You don't have to serve me anything. We don't have that arrangement, do we?"

"An arrangement." She laughs. "Nicely put."

She sees a warm glow spread across his face. She likes a smart man.

He pours her a glass, pours his.

"But I thought . . ." she says.

"This is an exception, an occasion, meeting such a fine lady in what would otherwise be desolation. Though, as I'm sure you know, Needles has its modest fame. John Steinbeck himself reported that the Joad family stopped here."

"*Grapes of Wrath.*"

He corrects her. "*The Grapes of Wrath.*"

Nina nods and, taking her glass, looks at him over the rim. "A song: 'I headed for Las Vegas, only made it out to Needles.'"

His head lolls back. "Ah," he says, coming forward, index finger up. "'Never Been to Spain.' The group?"

"Three Dog Night. I've had it blasting away all day."

"Never mind," says Louis Shaw.

"Never mind?"

"A hit in, what would you say, the 1970s?" He touches the rim of his glass to hers. "To success."

Nina sits upright in her chair. "Success in what?"

He cocks an eye. "Finding whatever you're after."

"What makes you think I'm after anything?"

"'Never been to heaven—'" He's quoting the song again.

She laughs and holds out her glass for more.

The cactus wren, an insect in its curved bill, scoots across the ditch to the brush on the other side. Nina notices a segment of barbed wire fence she hadn't seen before.

Louis Shaw says, "I surmise you've intuited that I'm a man who can't control his words. Why did you offer the wine? You weren't frightened? Insulted by my remark?"

She feels the buzz. "No." She was flattered in the skewed way that happens in between the times you know what you're doing.

"At our age," he says, "we haven't time to waste."

"Indeed." She rethinks his plainspoken words. *I want to*

make love to you. She misses sex. She glances across at the man who knows she's looking. He's put his glass on her camper step, taken off his hat to fan a fly away from his face. She wonders what his penis is like. She thinks about the shapes and textures of some she's known. One blunt, fat, and rubbery as a wine stopper. Another sharp, with that mean little curve that the man liked to use, holding her up so that her back arched and he could see the shape of the head of his penis inside her. How thin she was then, all hip bones and a recessive pelvic floor. The one that felt too thin, too long, her vagina unable to get a grasp on him, slippery in other ways too. She had loved looking at the penises, lifting them to study the undersides. It seemed a miracle of construction, the way a penis connected to the testicles and the testicles connected themselves to the body.

The cactus wren, perched on a eucalyptus in the distance, calls in its harsh, unmusical syllable that starts low and gathers speed. When she does go home to Oregon, she will miss the sound of that bird.

The air has cooled. Trucks rumble past with running lights on. Nina touches her shoulder. A star is working at being seen. She looks across at Louis Shaw, who smiles as though he shares her thoughts. She nods, acknowledging that he, too, has a history.

His fingers mesh to keep the twitch at bay. "I want," he says. "I am compelled to say it again. I want to make love to you."

She understands that he has a tic and that he is not a

dangerous man and that his words mean merely the natural connection between a man and a woman. "I can imagine it," she says. "You would be good." She drinks. Whatever attempt at sex she and this odd man might undertake would be memorable only in the odours and awkwardness, the ordeal of removing underwear in such a small space, the two of them struggling.

"In Oklahoma, in Arizona, what does it matter?" She moistens her lips, settles back in the chair. Says, "Oh, God." She holds the glass in front of her face to keep back a wayward laugh. "Oh, God," she says, closing her eyes.

He makes a sound like a chuckle. His mirthful sound, a burble of good feeling, makes her smile. The cactus wren picks up the pace with its *cha cha cha*. A light goes on in the Prowler. A rustle of warm wind lifts her hair.

She wakes early, dabs the grit out of her eyes with water, runs her fingers through her hair, smears on a pinkish lip coating, and steps outside. The Prowler is gone, as she knew, of course, it would be. "This ain't no thinking thing, no left brain or right . . ." Country songs, she's finding, give solace and advice. She throws the chocks in the bin, checks the hitch and stabilizer, and heads for the California coast, to find a special place at the ocean, another request of Miriam's.

Nina dries a brush with a rag and lays it by her paint box, lifts the phone, and dials. Waiting for Miriam to pick up, she looks out at the sky above the roof next door, a riotous blue, streaky with clouds. Mourning doves coo and strut on eaves. The phone on the other end rattles. Nina waits. She listens to her mother's breathing. Nina asks, "Are the birds at the feeder yet?"

"I'm taking my time this morning."

"Are the finches there yet?"

"I don't know."

The feeders are new. Nina put them up for her mother's amusement. "Can't you see them from your chair?"

Now Miriam isn't talking.

"Mother?"

"I'm in bed."

"Why are you in bed?" Nina knows why Miriam is still in bed. Parkinson's is building in her brain like the flow of bad news on TV.

"Never mind," her mother says. Hangs up.

Nina has rented a one-room apartment, close to Miriam, the travel trailer parked out back. She glances at her easel, a water-colour sketch of the Catalina Mountains with a focus on Table Rock. She did it *plein-air*. Not bad, but she has yet to capture the quiet observance, some as-yet-undefined quality inherent in them that makes your eyes look up. Wherever you are in Tucson, you are aware of the Catalinas. She dials again, takes a breath. "Is now the time? Should we go now?"

"Yes."

Online, Nina reads: "The Gentle-Ride Suspension U-Haul moving trucks ensure that even your most delicate possessions benefit from gentle cross-town or cross-country transportation." She loves the phrase "even your most delicate possessions." Frank would laugh. She drives over to the U-Haul outlet, signs the papers to rent the seventeen-foot Easy Loader, the cargo van with the widest and shortest ramp. She practises driving in a supermarket lot. Inside the supermarket, she steers a cart through the aisles, buying supplies.

Miriam has told Nina that she "just wants to look at the ocean one last time" before being carted down the hall to seriously assisted living, the part of the residence where they put you in diapers, she says, because it's less trouble for them than to inch you to the bathroom every—oh, in Miriam's case, every hour, and that's on a good day. If Nina will only drive her out of the desert, across the Laguna Mountains, west to San Diego and north to a secret cove Nina found, Miriam will say her farewells to the ocean. Nina has discovered that everyone who lives in the desert dreams of the ocean. She imagines Miriam has in mind the scene from the movie *Little Big Man*, the one where the tired old chief climbs a hill, says his prayers, and waits to die. Instead, it starts to rain and the old man gets up. Miriam probably believes her own plan will work, due to her especially strong will. She'll sit in her chair, the oak chair with legs ending in toes of lions; she's already told Nina that much. The feel of the sea rising and falling, swirling around her ankles and feet, no matter the condition of those feet—the bunions, the scabs, the gnarly ingrown nails—none of this will matter, because when the first wave breaks, Nina imagines that Miriam believes she will be cured of this life and die. "Ah," Miriam says and closes her eyes.

"Are you practising?"

"What? What? I'm an old woman half asleep."

Nina is perched on the ottoman changing the batteries in Miriam's TV remote. "I'm hoping we see a green flash." She visualizes a riotous, no-holds-barred sunset for Miriam, with that special spark at the end, a flash of green as the sun disappears over the horizon.

"What? What?"

Nina interprets these grunts as questions. "A green flash is when the refractive light ... curvature of the earth ..." She stumbles around in the definition. Frank would explain it so charmingly a kindergarten child could understand.

"I miss him too, you know," Miriam says as Nina hands her the remote.

Nina's eyes smart at the suddenness of Miriam's statement. She recalls a couple she met on the Oregon coast, checking out of the motel the day after they'd arrived. The woman, wearing a head bandage and an eye patch, had brain cancer. Too tired for a vacation. "God's will," her husband had said. Nina waved goodbye and ran, frantic and beside herself, across the sand to the ocean's edge, where she railed against

God. As the sun slid below the horizon, she saw a green flash.

Miriam is pounding her little fists on the chair. "I have never in all my years of living on the ocean seen a green flash." Miriam was raised in Washington State on the Olympic Peninsula, and to hear her tell it, she practically lived at the beach. Nina has heard the stories many times, the families— cousins, friends—packing the cart with real dishes, real silver, the horses and their driver arriving after the Studebakers. Summer at the shore, in tents. Under umbrellas, the women fanned their plump faces while the children played in the sand. The men returned to the camp on weekends.

"Maybe this time," Nina says. The slatted blinds at the open balcony door rustle. The air smells of orange blossom.

It's mighty strange for a U-Haul the size of the one Nina rented to show up at the residence entryway when no one has died and a family isn't hauling out furniture. The patients parked in their wheelchairs in the shade of olive and ash trees think they may have missed some news: "George was watching the TV one minute, then gone the next." That's the story they like to hear.

Nina carries an empty suitcase up the carpeted elevator to her mother's room, packs the clothing Miriam has managed to lay out, sweeps the counter of creams, lipsticks, and the pastes to hold teeth in, and treks down. Up again, she drags the chair with the lions' feet to the elevator, and sails down. Her mother's chair has a broad, strong stance and a tight, black leather seat cushion. She pulls it up the ramp, into the back of the van.

"There," she says to those gathered.

"You need to bungee it," an old man points out, finger shaking.

Nothing gets past these people, but Nina has thought of that too, as well as two single foam mattresses, bedding, pillows, a porta-potty with stabilizers, and a cooler loaded with bourbon that her mother likes, with water, and vodka and tonic for herself. Crackers. Wheat thins, her mother's favourite. Saltines. Smoked oysters, toothpicks. Cottage cheese with pineapple pieces. A jar of pickled eggs.

The group watches as Nina helps Miriam out of her wheelchair, pushes the chair up the ramp, and straps it down. Nina brings a step stool around to assist Miriam into the van. When her mother is settled in the passenger seat, there's a smattering of applause from those not holding on to walkers. By now, jokes fly about Miriam's journey.

"I'm serious!" Miriam says, her voice thready. But they get it. The ocean is everyone's dream. Some even belong to the Neptune Society, an organization that will come for your ashes, wherever they wind up, and take them out to sea.

"Bon voyage!" Miriam's friend calls. "I hope I never see you again."

"I should be so lucky!"

"You two are sounding like an old Jack Lemmon movie," Nina says.

Five miles along, they get stuck in traffic on the way to the I-10.

Miriam says, "I'm thirsty."

Nina remembers Miriam saying her bladder is the size of a pea. She says, "No water until we get somewhere."

Miriam laughs.

They spend a night in a motel in Yuma. They can hear dune buggies buzzing most of the night. Driving west again, between pleasant silences their conversation is sketchy. Nina asks, "Do you want a new set of sheets when you move? I can get the ones with flowers if you like."

"No. Too cute   get something else."

"I brought an   gant taupe for the camp-out."

"Goody," Miriam says.

Over the Laguna Mountains, past splashes of daisy-like yellow wildflowers: "Are you going to miss the tapestry sofa?" Miriam's assisted living suite will be smaller.

"I bought it after the divorce. I thought it had class. What did I know? I've hated it for years."

"You didn't tell me."

"You had a busy life."

Frank again. "Yes," Nina says.

Traffic jams in San Diego, the sky a gauzy blot, tail lights for miles: "From the sounds of it, you didn't choose much in life."

Miriam snorts. "Life happens. Then one day you choose the ocean."

Nina manoevres around another moving truck the size of hers. The whole state is restless.

"I didn't choose to live in a room with my name on the door, either," Miriam says. "In case you're wondering."

They stay in a hotel on the ocean, one that Miriam says is "fancy." They eat filet mignon and scallops for dinner. The meal makes Miriam's digestion uneasy, but she says the taste was worth it. She trots to the toilet so fast her walker barely touches ground. The next morning, room service brings breakfast and Miriam is back to plain oatmeal, albeit garnished with a nasturtium.

Nina carries the heavy oak chair, propped against her hip, to where foam fans the beach. The air is tangy with hints of sea-weed. Miriam waits at the U-Haul, tucked along a gravelly spot in a cove. When Nina returns, Miriam leans on her and moves toward the sea, groaning, which hurts Nina's heart. Miriam settles in the chair, the breeze catches her thinning hair and the surf swirls around her bare ankles. Soon her feet are buried in sand; she makes a squat silhouette—a perfect photo if you were standing far enough back—and out beyond her, a generous but ordinary orange sunset, smeary due to haze and smog.

Later, Nina and Miriam lay side by side, mattresses on the ramp, their heads on goose-down pillows. Miriam settles with a sigh, bony fingers caressing the wonderful sheets. The last gulls cry, stars glisten. They hear the rhythmic rumbling of waves. "Thank you," Miriam says. The jaw lets go its grip. Miriam letting go causes Nina to lie awake, tears drying on her cheeks. She adores her mother's whistling snores. Frank would love this story.

Back at the retirement complex, an audience has gathered to see Miriam in her new digs. She's down to one room and a bathroom. "New wing, new view, less housekeeping," Miriam says. She's in her chair, salt stains on its legs, and behind her, on the shelf, her prized blue and white Ming-style vase. She is dressed, as she would say, to the nines, her hair freshly permed. Nina is serving tea on TV trays. She's brought chairs for the guests from the nearby dining room.

"You don't look transformed to me, kiddo," says one of Miriam's friends.

Miriam pauses to look around the room, her chin raised. Gradually people hush each other and turn toward her. Miriam makes her announcement: "I have seen the green flash."

Nina raises her eyebrows.

"It was a miracle, a sunset to end all sunsets." Miriam's lips may slide over consonants, but in her unwavering gaze is the glory of the green flash captured at long last. An old man wants to know what in tarnation a green flash is.

Nina says, "Well, it's refracted light—" Miriam coughs into the back of her hand. Nina stops talking and passes a bowl of oatmeal cookies. Eager hands reach out. She locks eyes with her mother. Miriam gives her the thumbs-up.

Nina hands the bowl with what's left of the cookies to the old man. His eyes blink with pleasure. She walks around so she can stand behind Miriam's chair and places her hands on her mother's shoulders. She clears her throat. "It was unbelievably lucky," she says. "We parked in the perfect cove and had plenty of time to get out to where the sand meets the waves." Then, to satisfied murmurs and munching and sighs, Nina paints the scene. Describes a gull wrestling with a saltine wrapper, pelicans at dusk in formation above the dappled sea, and the moment the sun, the rich, deep colour of a tangerine, dropped from sight, a miraculous spark of green flashed on the horizon, like a wink.

Bingo

Driving on a freeway in central California amid cattle trailers and freight trucks bound for Sacramento, Mary noticed a softening in her chest, the only warning that tears were on their way; one of her crying jags was coming on. She missed her mother and, incongruously, missed her mother's ancient cat, with its ratty, patchy fur. By the time Mary moved back into her mother's house—her mother preferred to be called Mrs. Garrity—to look after her when the Alzheimer's became incapacitating, the calico tabby (never in the best of moods even as a kitten, as Mary recalled) had become grouchy and cantankerous. After Mrs. Garrity died, the cat had hissed at Mary as though it was her fault. Mary's intervention hadn't made a life-changing difference to her mother or the cat; they carried on, as usual, their mutual complaints like a moaning Greek chorus, a backdrop to Mary's cheery, high-strung helpfulness.

She signalled, batted her arm around in the hard wind out the window for emphasis, and pulled over, the brakes on the travel trailer squealing. A smell of burnt rubber rose up. She crept along the shoulder to the rest stop, where she slipped in between the big-rig cargo trucks. She was exhausted and had let herself run out of propane—without propane the fridge and stove wouldn't work. The rest stop had the basics, restrooms and snack machines.

Yes, she was glad her mother was gone; Alzheimer's takes a terrible toll. But whenever she had told anyone, whenever she had spoken that simple truth out loud, heat rose to her cheeks and the words felt reprehensible, as though her time in the pit—her two years of dealing with the bathing, insults, tantrums, and doing her best—didn't count.

Mary lay on the bed strewn with open state maps and a Woodall's camping guide, and cried and blew her nose. Whenever she managed to focus on precisely where she might be, the sobbing would begin again.

After two Snickers bars, a 7UP, a bag of chips, five hours of listening to the whine of generators keeping produce cool, and the screech of air brakes as trucks drove in and out, her tears dried up and her vision cleared. She was staring at an RV map of central California when she realized that down the road a few miles south, a stone's throw away, an RV camp awaited, a camp situated on the Sacramento River.

It was a hallelujah moment. The nature of suffering—she had worked her way through two boxes of tissue—is that you can't see beyond it. Misery exists to make you truly miserable. Thinking these thoughts, she climbed back onto the freeway, joined in the flow, and pulled off a few exits later. She drove under the freeway and onto a country road lined with sycamore and eucalyptus trees, with fields beyond. She followed the signs, made a wide turn, and took a small road down a hill. At the bottom was a little clapboard office that needed paint.

Outside, a tall man pruning the bushes laid down the clippers, wiped his brow, and sauntered over to her window. "Welcome." He introduced himself as Ben Erickson, camp manager. He had tousled brown hair and, to her surprise, a missing incisor. She had seen plenty of missing teeth in eastern Oregon and other rural areas but never in California. Mary had to hold back tears because he was so friendly despite her being red-eyed and dishevelled—even her nose felt swollen. He filled her propane tanks and then she went inside and signed the register, handed over her credit card. She bought a bag of peanuts and two frozen dinners, not a great nutritional start, but a start.

Apparently she'd arrived at a lucky time. Any earlier and he wouldn't have had a space for her, but a spot right on the river had just opened up. He was putting her next to a Sundance. He warned her that the couple that owned the Sundance was here due to their twenty-four-year-old lad who'd been in a skateboarding accident and was now in a coma in hospital. "You seem like a respectful sort of person," Ben said.

Mary backed into the spot assigned her and did the hookups quietly. She set up her awning, laid out the patio mat and a couple of folding chairs. Over the next few days the couple from the Sundance came and went, driving an old Dodge. Sometimes a girl, the girlfriend of the skateboarder, Mary learned, went with them.

Mary was outside cleaning her binoculars when the couple dropped by. "We'll look after our Nicky, no matter what," the mother told Mary. "If only God will let him live." She had especially big eyes—a thyroid problem, Mary guessed—and the boy's father, a small-boned man, wept quietly, his eyes spilling tears. Mary said she understood. They got in their car and drove away. A blue heron flew down the wide river, the colour a seasoned sage green, the current strong and steady. The fisherman who was out with his rod when she first arrived and on other afternoons, a fat, freckled man fly-casting from the shore, tried again. Every afternoon the man nodded at Mary and she would raise her hand, give a cautious wave back.

By then Mary knew that the girlfriend was named Tammy. The girl, Mary noticed, would pace around the Sundance and sometimes farther afield, but always within one section of the camp, as though confined by an invisible fence. Sometimes, when the parents weren't there, she turned the TV up loud.

One day she stopped by Mary's and asked, "How long you going to stay?"

"Dunno," said Mary. "This is a nice place."

"We might be here forever." Tammy looked like a waif, thin with bony little fingers. She had tattoos of rose vines up both arms.

"Have a seat. Want a beer?" Mary handed her a Miller from the cooler.

Tammy sat on the camper step. "I was gonna leave him. Just before the accident."

"Oh, no. Now you're stuck."

"Looks that way." Tammy's stringy yellow hair had a fading ruby stripe running through it. "I sort of thought it was him," she said. She meant the man she was waiting for, the one who wanted something better than Yuba City, the man who would take her to Frisco. Now, she wasn't sure which way to pray. "About him. You know. Nicky. Should he get better? Or, uh, the other. He might be, well, in bad shape." She'd given up her job at a restaurant called Weatherbee's and moved out of the apartment she and Nicky shared with another twosome.

In Mary's world, there weren't many available men, though occasionally she had fantasies that one would come along who would find her compact, nearly sixty body, with its easygoing, ample boobs, appealing. "Listen." She took aim at the girl. "If you don't love this guy enough, get out now." The words sounded harsh, and hearing them, Mary felt her cheeks redden.

"You think?" Tammy ducked her head, glanced over at the empty Sundance, the faded plaid curtains at the slider window tied back tidily. The cottonwood trees shifted overhead; raucous cries of mating green herons competed with the fast, wide river coursing beneath a slight wind. The fat man cast his line again. "They're nice to me," Tammy said of her boyfriend's parents.

"Yep."

"What do you mean?"

"They're going to need help changing the diapers." Mary thought back. Her mother had come down with senility as though it was a cold that would pass. Some sputtering attempts at finding words, asking which way to the bathroom, and a peculiar incident, the cans of tamales hidden under her bed. Then it seemed to blow over. Mrs. Garrity recovered, so Mary thought, until she asked about the tamales. "I ate tamales when I was pregnant with you. I ate them cold out of the can; I was addicted to the texture of the cornmeal and the slippery red grease. The social worker caught me. I said, 'Protein,' and she said nothing, just backed out of the house. The house was a rental in Florida. I can't remember the name of the town. I didn't think loving tamales was that strange, but you never know what other people think. She had a clipboard in her hand, and I never saw her again."

Mrs. Garrity wasn't her biological mother—Mary was adopted—nor had Mrs. Garrity ever lived in Florida, so far as

Mary knew. Mary had the camper parked in the driveway when she found the cans and heard the story about the tamales. She brought her clothes into the house and moved into her old room, painted an enthusiastic, oppressive gold, like being buried inside a bouquet of slightly old, store-bought chrysanthemums.

It was a slow death, Mary staring into eyes that would suddenly change from calm blue pools with no glimmer to brown swirling tide pools crazy with anger. Mrs. Garrity would strike out and try to hit Mary. Mary had to slap her once to get her to calm down. The old cat would slither out from under the couch and join in, yowling. Then, within seconds of the outrage and destructive behaviour, Mrs. Garrity would cry out and sink to a chair, feeble and confused. Bowel incontinence would follow. Mary looked sideways at Tammy and thought about Nicky. "Diapers," she said.

"Oh, shit. I never thought about that part. You sure?"

"No."

"Omigod." Tammy sucked the beer down, placed the empty on Mary's step. "I can't do that. I just can't. I was leaving him anyway. He wouldn't get a job. He was just, like, into skating."

Mary stood. "Find a trucker without a wife living in the cab. Stay away from ones with dogs. There's a truckers' rest stop a few miles north. Most of them are gentle men. Bound to be a Weatherbee's down the road."

The girl squinted at Mary and wobbled in her blocky sandals. "But he loves me," she said.

"A problem," said Mary.

Later, Mary wandered around the park, carrying her binoculars. Sometimes she thought her binoculars were a cover for snooping around in other people's business. Here, however, she was simply taken with the mating green herons.

The new arrivals on Mary's other side were drinking all afternoon, beer and glasses of white Zinfandel. They showed up on a Friday and set out a green golf rug, three chairs, two tables, and a palm tree the height of their rig, with lights on it. "We're on a long weekend away, just the two of us," explained the man with a white goatee. "She likes to get out. We live 'bout thirty miles toward town, but this here, this here is wilderness, so we like it."

Mary eyed the electric palm tree.

"Pretty, in't it? She chose it."

"There's a whole river right here, with real birds and trees," Mary said.

He shrugged.

Their dog was a Chihuahua named Princess. The dog's name was sewn in pink and purple sequins on a small canvasback chair.

"Isn't she just a love?" the woman said to Mary.

"Chair is cute all right. Have a good one."

In the trees above the get-away couple, the green herons, usually elusive birds, were making primitive, ecstatic jumps at each other. Leaves rustled, marking their excitement.

Mary overheard the man say, "Are you still cranky?" The country station played "Livin' Our Love Song"—again, third time in an hour, by Mary's reckoning. A woodpecker drummed on a pole, and a cormorant flew above the river in the other direction. Over by the laundry shack, in the tree, House finches were mating. The male stiffened his wings, lunged, pinned the female. Princess snoozed in her chair.

Mary walked past a row of campers to the clubhouse, a blocky stucco building separate from the office. Dee Erickson, who managed the place with Ben, told her that owls nested in a big hole in a valley oak and starlings were higher up. Dee was on the lawn, throwing plastic bones to their black Labs. She glanced at the oak and said to Mary, "I thought of poisoning those damn starlings. You seen the screech owls yet?"

"Nah," said Mary. The owls would be Western screech owls, a bird she'd never seen—a lifer for her list if she saw one. She said, "Came to check last night but missed them. Most people don't know starlings are invasive, but you do."

"I know more than I look like I know." Dee had a big laugh. "I used to teach biology at the college near Santa Barbara. Ben had some big ideas about real estate."

Trailing spider webs floated between the valley oak and the sycamore. Ben and Dee had two grown girls, one married with a baby, one at university. To keep the one girl in school, they'd sold everything and put off Ben's dental work.

In the bushes Mary spotted a pair of Bullock's orioles, their bodies the colour of oranges, their eyes rimmed in black to go with their black throats.

"Here's a true story," Dee said, patting one of the dogs. "I was meeting Ben in Vancouver, staying at The Sylvia, by the water. You know the place?"

Mary nodded. The Sylvia, on English Bay, was a quaint old hotel with tiny rooms and windows that opened to real air. She'd stayed there once with a friend, when she had friends, before the Alzheimer's took hold of her mother. Funny how that went; people got tired of you complaining about how your mother told the same stories over and over again, as you yourself went on and on. Mary nodded at Dee again.

"So Ben's conference was over the next day. And there I was, in the room, a day early. A gull flew in the open window, and sat on the table and watched me eat dinner. A hot dog, something simple. I said to it, 'Ben won't believe this, so please come back in the morning.' I phoned Ben, said the bird would see him in the morning. In the morning it came back, sat at the table in the same place. Ben opened the door and just started laughing."

"I think you're a bird psychic." Mary laughed.

"She is." Ben walked up, smiling, and patted one of the Labs.

The three of them followed the dogs down the trail to the river.

"You want to hear my theory about how birds find their way?" Ben asked.

"He should have been the biologist, instead of an engineer," Dee said, watching the Labs splashing in the river, pouncing in and out.

"Here's my theory." Ben rubbed his palms together. "Birds have a different schema of seeing. They analyze everything through colour. They have fluorescent sight, so to birds the female is striking, whereas all we see is plainness. Same with mountains. Birds see the colour deep inside the rocks of deserts and mountains. They see blazes of deep colour that translate into a map of light in their brains, and that light leads them where they need to go."

"Home," Dee said. She took his arm.

"Anywhere you are, hon," he said. "I made mistakes," he told Mary. "I lost the house. I lost everything we had."

"Yeah, but, hey, unlike a house, trailers don't take much time to clean so I have energy to burn." Dee laughed. "We could go fuck our brains out right about now, but bingo starts at seven."

"Bingo is my burden," Ben said. "The one thing about this job I hate. I make 'em wait 'til 7:06."

"They're not bad people," Dee said. "Wanna come play?"

Mary shook her head no. She had played plenty of bingo when Mrs. Garrity could still play.

She watched Dee and Ben strolling away. Dee's head touched Ben's shoulder, moved back and touched him again, like nuzzling. The dogs shook themselves, a spiral head-to-toe shimmy that efficiently removed water from their coats. Then

Mary was alone on the lawn, standing so still it felt like meditation. She glanced at the hole where the screech owls nested. Not a chance in hell she would see them, not with her luck. A gull landed on the trail to the beach—she identified it, tentatively, as a ring-billed; gulls were hard to positively ID because they passed through so many phases to maturity. The gull waddled toward her, its yellow eye bright, acquisitive, as though Mary might have a sausage roll in her hand, or the last chewy bite of a hot-dog bun.

The gull came to within two feet of her.

Mary asked, "Were you once in Vancouver?"

The bird muttered something and glided away.

Mary turned around and saw the girl, Tammy, walking up the road, a duffle bag slung over her shoulder. There was only one road in, and the same road out. Mary gulped air. Her eyes smarted. If she raised her arms, she might fly.

Dee appeared from the back door of the clubhouse to pick up a dog toy. Her gaze followed Mary's. "Young to be so burdened."

"Maybe not," Mary said. "Maybe not burdened anymore."

"It's bingo time," Dee said. "You sure you won't come?"

"No," Mary said. "Actually, I'm not sure at all."

She followed Dee inside and found a chair in the back row. Someone bumped past her, slid a warm paw across her shoulders on the way to a seat beside her.

Mary noticed the man's big freckled hands and his face glistening in the humid air. "You catch anything?"

"Not yet." He bumped her arm with his elbow. "I don't usually do this. But get ready, girl. You're sitting next to the big-boy winner!"

"Hell, no," Mary said. "This night's mine."

On the dais, Ben made a trumpet sound out of the corner of his mouth, like the start of a horse race, or a rooster with a warbled crow. Someone laughed. Ben opened his mouth, showed his missing tooth. "You retired, easygoing RV folk ready for a good time?" He used an accent Mary hadn't heard before—the cost of being partly an entertainer for a living, she supposed. Dee shrugged as though Ben was out of her control. The ladies in front tittered. Beer tops popped. The air from the Sacramento River was sweet.

Little Dove

Delphinium is not a happy cat. Partly, Linda thinks, he must hate his name. She's tried calling him Del, but when she does he won't even turn his head in her direction. She inherited the cat when she rented the single wide trailer west of Tucson. Delphinium is a short-haired tabby with a restless orange tail. He's twitchy. Right now he's twitchy because the mourning doves that nest on the roof of the trailer next door have at least one fledgling and the fledgling is in the mesquite tree staring at Delphinium, and Delphinium, she sees, is plotting.

"You!" She slides open the window and gives a shout. The cat's eyes widen. The dove puffs its body up, as though it's big.

"God." Linda slams the window shut. She hurries to the door, flings herself out, and jumps off the porch, but by the time she makes it over the wire fence (the part the javelinas, a species of wild pig that roams the Sonoran desert, have wrecked) and into the vacant lot, Delphinium is long gone and the baby bird is now staring at her.

"Cats can climb trees," she tells the dove. "Where's your brother?" Doves are prolific in southern Arizona. Usually they lay two eggs at a time, but the parents of this silly thing gazing saucer-eyed at her from the tree may be exhausted; they've had a pair of fledglings already this season. Maybe this one is on its own.

The finches and siskins have scattered from her feeder; she's scared them. They're hiding in the thickets of brush, waiting. She doesn't worry about Delphinium catching one of them; when birds know where a cat lives, they will tease it by diving low or gang up on it, chittering as though they're laughing.

Three children from her church will be over after school for an art lesson. Linda teaches Crayon Crazy! on her covered porch. She bought a heavy steel table and keeps the crayons, paper, and other tools in a locked box under it. She teaches the children to make layers of colour so that their work looks jewel-like, sometimes like an oil painting. The two boys in her class are seven-year-old twins, and the girl is nine. Today she'll be showing them how to texture, using woodcarving tools she bought at a second-hand store. The tools are well used, not especially sharp. She runs her hand over the oilcloth on the table, brushing off dirt. The slightest wind coats everything with a fine grey powder.

After lunch, she drives her car over to the bagel shop and parks out front. She feels like a criminal, sitting with her computer in her lap, but the bagel shop is also tainted—it moved into town under the guise of an independent business, but turns out to be part of a chain, a sly one. Linda doesn't like their bagels, but occasionally, out of courtesy for the Internet access, she buys something.

It's an intensely white April day, not bright, just an eye-aching white, the beginning of summer. By mid-May it will be scorching, and in June even hotter, the land drier. The monsoons start in July. By September it's fall, and in late December, the birds start mating. Linda's had to relearn the seasons; the prairies, where she's from, function on an entirely different schedule.

She sits in her Hyundai and scrolls through videos and jokes people feel they just have to share, and then her fingers stop, because her old friend Irene has sent a message. At first she thinks it's a mistake. She must have read it wrong. She looks again. There it is: "Anthony was hit by a car, they say he didn't suffer. Bawling my head off."

Linda covers her eyes with her hands. The image of a little boy running after a ball and a car, like a nightmare, coming.

Linda closes the lid of the laptop, closes her eyes. Her heart begins to race. She thinks she might faint. Anthony is Irene's only grandchild.

At five a child is interested in everything, he is past clinging to baby ways, he has stepped up to the plate as a human, yet is still charming if there's a reward. He knows things but doesn't know too much. He knows when you're really fed up or just pretending to be. He has the grace to go along with you, not argue when he knows you're sad. The embedded kindness in the human heart shows up well in a child of five.

Back home, she scrubs the kitchen floor on her hands and knees and then goes to the file cabinet and chooses a four-by-six-inch card she's made—crayon-painted—for a sympathy note to Irene's daughter. She's known Irene's daughter since she was small. She didn't want a baby, but her boyfriend did and so Anthony was born, and Irene was filled with joy to be given this angel from heaven.

Anthony—never Tony—was bright-eyed and darling. Linda has a file of pictures Irene e-mailed over the years, and on a shelf nearby, the photo album of her own precious child with his gassy, newborn smile. She has pictures of him until the age of five.

Irene's answering machine *beep-beeps*, won't let Linda leave a message. Maybe she's had so many calls it's filled up. Or Irene has unplugged it. Linda remembers herself unplugging every-thing—the answering machine, the phone, the radio, the TV, too many reminders of life going on, as though there could possibly be a reason.

She stands with her palms on the kitchen table and studies the card. She glances at the clock, aware of her little class later in the day. The picture on the card is a path in the woods, a hint of light in the distance.

Who dies at five?

The pee arcing into the room from the bassinet made Linda and the little squirt's father laugh. They were twenty-two years old, both of them, and had married at city hall because the baby was obviously on the way and her husband's parents, Catholics, wanted them married. "Watch your back," she said to her new husband. "He'll be a big pisser pretty soon." The baby didn't understand what he'd done but was pleased by their reaction. Her husband's face glowed with love for his boy. This baby. Created in her body. Created in a moment of lust. Or maybe during make-up sex because they fought a lot, over money, about him spending too much time watching sports with the guys. It might have happened as they snuggled, exhausted from moving into a little house from an apartment, and rolled into lovemaking, his powerful legs spreading hers. The perfect little pisser conceived that night.

Children bloom everywhere, but there is that one child who is yours, and he is funny and smart, even if he is a pain in the ass at times. Linda's child had fevers and sweats, but all children did. Daddy ran the bath. "Not too cold," she pleaded. This happened when the two of them were still speaking. The fever turned out to be nothing, a childhood thing. Children have these episodes all the time, they said at the hospital. Then the child turned pale again, wouldn't eat meat, wasn't getting enough iron, hated scrambled eggs. She tried various foods, and he refused them, and then she put him on children's chewable vitamins.

It is the nature of the human body to thrive and grow, and surely this one would too, the slight body of her small-boned child.

She wipes the tears from her cheeks; they appear without warning. She takes out the shoebox she keeps in a bottom drawer, sits on a cushion on the floor, and sifts through clippings, the overhead fan *lop-lopping*, stirring heat. One day it will fall on her head. In Phoenix, a sleeping three-year-old died of hyperthermia, left in a car in the summer heat while his mom shopped. In Wisconsin, a five-year-old was run over by a tractor driven by his ten-year-old cousin. A bucking horse threw its rider off, and the little girl died from head trauma. That was in Nevada.

Reading the clippings—children die every day—calms her.

Back at the table she reads her note: *I was very sorry to hear about the loss of your child. Death is terrible when it takes someone so young. I know from experience it will not be easy to get over.* She picks up the pen, a Zeb Roller 2000. It's leaky and smudges the edge of letters—just look at the *D* in *Death*. *With sympathy and thinking of you.* She blows on the ink, wonders if her words are helpful or cruelly honest. Or just cruel.

She wants to smoke a cigarette; she wants to be pacified by a cigarette. She used to love them, no matter what anyone said. Then she quit, as part of the punishment.

Her little boy used to snuff out their cigarettes with a rock he kept in his pocket, going from her ashtray to his dad's muttering, "Tut, tut, tut"—where in the world did he learn that? He grew into a playful child, despite the ongoing battles between his parents. He'd call from the bedroom, "Can you guys keep it down out there? I'm trying to think," and one particularly bad night he came twirling out of his room, dancing to music in his head, turning and bowing and flipping his top hat from Halloween. That show had shut them up.

She opens the refrigerator, leans in. The cool air feels good. She retrieves a no-name cola. She sits at the table on the chair with the tasselled pillow, gulps from the can. The cola fizzles into her throat and into her nose. Her colleagues and friends from those days are gone. You leave the child's father, leave the block, leave everything behind, as though the loss will stay behind.

The days and months when she had a child who slowly died

are gone. He was five; he was sixty-four months and three days old. It wasn't neglect, just medical ignorance about side effects, of how the kidneys could just give up.

No one said life would be fair.

She wonders if Irene was drinking while babysitting, wonders if Irene fell asleep. Then she wonders why she has such a heartless streak to imagine such a fault in a friend.

You always think it's your fault. It stays your fault. Time has passed, yet God is still far away. If Irene had so much as one drink, she will blame herself.

Delphinium throws himself against the outside of the door.

She opens the bottom drawer again, pulls from it her child's baby blanket. She lays herself on the couch, on top of the soft wool blanket, aware of her bare arms and how wool irritates her, how it itches and sets up reactions on the inside of her that make her want to curl her nails and go at it.

Why, for all this suffering, hasn't she become a better person?

Delphinium thuds against the door again, gives up.

She sets the carton of apple juice on the table and lines up the little glasses they like. The children are thirsty after school; they need sugar. They're on time, and noisy as they step over the crushed fence onto her patio. They've found a mourning dove on the ground, in the empty lot. The girl holds the fledgling in both hands, so that the dove's blank little head pokes out. "Oh, my gosh," Linda says. "That's him. I know that bird."

She will kill Delphinium the next time she sees him.

One of the twins says, "I bet Del—your cat—I bet your cat got it."

"Naw." His brother shakes his head. "It's right here. It's not dead, either."

Linda blinks. The child is right. The bird isn't dead—it is right here staring at her. She runs inside and hurries back out with a deep, stainless steel cooking pot and some dishtowels. The little girl places the dove inside and lets go. Linda reaches in, works her fingers gently over the fledgling's body. Then she lays a dishtowel over the pot. The smallest twin opens the door so she can take the bird inside, away from the exuberant noise of the children chattering when they start colouring. The baby is in shock; it needs quiet. It will be in shock for a time, she knows from experience. But the little thing has all its feathers and two good legs. It has a strong heartbeat, and it has her. It has a chance.

Darling

❡

Evan's cat was named Darlene when she got her from the Humane Society of Southern Arizona, but Evan called her Darling. Over the phone she told Darling's story to her brother. Her brother's name was Eric, so growing up they had been Evan and Eric, like twin boys instead of brother and sister.

Darling was a tabby with black markings on the tips of her ears, giving her a lynx-like look, and she had a high rump and a stubby, corkscrewed tail. Thankfully, the tail was covered in a ball of fur. The shelter people said she looked like a Manx, and the comment made Evan feel proud, as though Darling's interesting appearance was her doing. Darling had been returned because she was "too busy" at night. Also, the previous owner had had a baby.

"Cat would probably maul that baby given a chance," Evan's brother said, on the phone from Indianapolis.

She hadn't thought of the possibility. "Domestic cats don't maul things." Then she looked at the bandages on her arms. From the beginning, Darling stalked her. Evan would be lying in bed, listening to soft movements in the room. Turning her head, she would see Darling crouched on the headboard staring crookedly down on her, yellow eyes rapt and spellbound like nothing domesticated. Sometimes the cat pounced, claws out. Evan would throw Darling off the bed like she was a rat attacking. "That's morbid," she said to Eric, thinking of a cat mauling a baby. "That's a morbid thing to say."

"I'm feeling morbid," her brother said. Recently Eric's wife, Cathy, had died of cancer. He'd been by her side, in and out of hospitals for a year.

"I'm sorry. Of course," Evan said. "How are you feeling?"

"Relieved. Guilty for feeling relieved. Lonely. Like shit."

Evan survived another day of substitute teaching. The door to her two-bedroom apartment opened onto the kitchen. She peeked in cautiously; Darling had once leapt at her from the top of the refrigerator. She put her bags on the counter and tiptoed into the bedroom. "Darling?" Darling was under the bed. Evan lay on the floor on her stomach and stretched out her hand. She whispered, "You are my darling, you want to be my darling," and Darling put a paw out toward Evan's fingers. Evan cooed "my darling," again and Darling allowed her paw to be touched. Evan, who had been spat at by a boy in the class earlier in the day, cried at the soft touch of the cat's paw.

Evan remembered reaching for the frying pan for effect during a fight, before her husband, Ray, had taken the Malibu and driven two hundred miles away from her, and then crashed the car against a rock face outside Gila Bend. He was a drunk, an alcoholic, chronically self-absorbed, and full of self-pity, none of which, she'd realized, was curable. She thanked God they'd had no children, but that meant she might not ever have any. They didn't have much love, either. They occasionally fell together into sex and wrestled on the bed. Their social inadequacies bonded them, as well as the need to analyze their mothers, their fathers, their brothers and sisters. They talked endlessly about the differences in Anglo and Mexican families but mostly about what made each of them so different, in attempts to put together the reasons why they had so few friends. Evan felt socially inept; she never said the right thing, laughed when others didn't, repeated things twice or three times if people seemed to like what she'd said. Then, invariably, she regretted saying anything. She jumped into conversations at the wrong moment so that people stopped speaking and gave her looks bordering on disdain. Ray was worse off; he couldn't hold a job. He was sure people were watching him and judging his every move. On the shop floor, always on the alert for criticism, he would burst out, blame another mechanic for what he felt was a slight.

After he died, people were curious about whether Ray's death was a suicide or whether alcohol was to blame, as though the two—the dark fury in him that caused him to drink—could be separated. Evan moved to north-central Tucson from the southeast side, to start a new life. The people she'd known in the southeast schools drifted away, as though she'd moved to the moon. Being a substitute teacher kept her an outsider in the staff room anyway, yet made her privy to the secrets in teachers' desk drawers, or their lax classroom discipline.

Her new apartment was on the bottom floor of a two-storey building, with a sliding glass door that opened to the small patio. The apartments, all in a row, looked out onto a deep wash, a run-off for water during heavy rains. Because the wash was left in its natural state, Evan was thrilled to realize that animals lived in it and passed through it. Javelinas trotted up from the wash and onto the pathway around the complex three or four times a week toward the end of the day. Javelinas, Evan read, belonged to the collared peccary family. Tough-hided and tough-minded, they moved in family groups. Evan heard they liked broccoli, so she tossed pieces of broccoli out for them. She was fascinated by them, took photos and sent cards to her husband's family (who weren't speaking to her), the principals of schools she subbed for, and her brother.

On a branch of the mesquite tree outside the next apartment, a quart-sized Mountain Dew bottle hung upside down. Up close, Evan saw that it had a wood dowel for a perch and holes where birds could get the seeds out. The neighbour from the apartment trundled out to hang a refilled hummingbird feeder, the red plastic kind with fake yellow flowers. The hummingbirds were hovering around, waiting. "Oh, you will love the birds! And the pop bottles are Joe's invention. He's married to an older woman, you know." Alma Carpenter said she was eighty-four years old.

Evan said, "I have a cat."

"Don't let it get at the birds. Except the roadrunner, an evil thing, the cat can have that damned thing. That evil roadrunner scrunched itself down small in that bush over there, and jumped out faster than lightning and swallowed a verdin, a sweet little yellow bird that was just coming down from the feeder. Just swooping down after a feed and, whack, was swallowed by that evil thing. Somebody down the way"—Evan looked along the row of apartments in the direction Alma indicated—"is a stupid fool, and feeds that damned thing hamburger."

"My cat stays inside. I had to promise the humane shelter. They don't want cats to get hurt by coyotes. And they love birds too, of course."

"Thank the Lord," said Alma. She took a carrot out of her apron pocket and placed it under the tree. "This is for the rabbit."

The Jack Russell in the fenced yard on the other side of Evan's apartment began to bark.

"That dog could use a muzzle," Alma said. She shook a finger at him. The Jack Russell barked harder. She glanced at Evan. "I have cookies in the oven, why don't you come in?"

Evan was delighted.

While eating oatmeal cookies with chocolate chips she found out that Joe and Alma had been married for sixty-two years, that he was three days younger than Alma, and that twelve years ago they started feeding carrots to the rabbits. "In the beginning," Joe said, "those dang things were so dumb they didn't know what was good for them."

Joe was a big man with dry lips. He was wearing a blue shirt that matched his eyes and red suspenders. His long face was blotched from sun and wind, Evan guessed, or just old age. "Alma here had to teach those rabbits the colour orange. Then they caught on, them and the squirrels and that there chipmunk." He walked to the sliding door and pointed out to Evan a big-eyed desert rabbit, hunched under the mesquite tree, eating the carrot. Next he pointed at a chipmunk waiting in the brush. "That little feller is a regular clown," Joe said. "They do this most every night. Like a regular TV show. That chipmunk will come out—" and Evan saw that the chipmunk did come out, he darted from under the brush, raced toward the rabbit. The rabbit jumped straight up, just as Joe said it would, and the chipmunk snatched the carrot. The rabbit landed and hopped around in a slow circle, looking for his carrot, puzzled. The chipmunk, meanwhile, had run back to the brush, where it snickered.

Evan bought a pair of binoculars and a birder's book and started ticking off birds: the tiny verdin with the little red shoulder patch, the evil roadrunner, the Costa's hummingbird, the Gambel's quail, and the swarms of mourning doves—"their wings sound beautiful when they take off or land," she wrote in small letters along the margin. A Gila woodpecker, red spot on his crown, figured out how to grasp the perch of the Mountain Dew bottle with his claws and do pull-ups to get his bill into the seeds. He clung upside down—toning his little abs—and flung seeds out recklessly. This exercise gave the impression of being hard for him; he didn't stay at it long. Evan wondered if he did it for the amusement of the mourning doves and the white-crowned sparrows below, happily squabbling and gobbling.

She phoned her brother to share the tales about mishaps in the wash that Joe had regaled her with. During monsoon season, rivers of water could come roaring along and overflow the washes. One year, a dumb Minnesota snowbird in an SUV figured he'd beat the water and was carried away, landing in mud two miles from where he'd started, upside down, with a broken collarbone. It happened frequently enough that, Evan remarked to her brother, a person just had to wonder about the intelligence of some people.

She explained the same thing to Darling. "You stay away if you see water whooshing in the wash." Darling, pressed to the sliding door, eyed the birds, her jaws jittering.

The next day, Evan planned to run into Alma as she was tossing the birdseed to tell her she loved Joe's stories. Alma, tiny chin twitching, murmured shyly, "You know Joe is married to an older woman."

"Oh, yes, I do know that," said Evan.

Feeling sleep deprived, Evan had the idea of making a nice nest for Darling in the spare room; the room had Evan's desk and computer, the litter box, and not much else in it. She arranged a nice set-up—Darling's treats, water and food, a cozy cat bed, even a radio turned to a station that played soothing music—said goodnight, and eased the door closed. Over several nights, Darling threw litter out of the box, spilled her water bowl, and batted her dry food around the floor; in the mornings the room looked like ten cats lived in it, and none of them with any manners.

Eventually she gave up trying to keep Darling confined at night. One night Evan rubbed her feet together under the sheets and instantly knew she'd made a mistake. A moment later, Darling pounced and grabbed a foot with her claws. "Ouch!" Evan yelled and kicked her feet in the air. She reached down and batted at the cat. Darling thumped to the floor. Evan heard her growling from under the bed and was afraid to get up. She squinted at the clock: 2:38 AM. While she waited for her heart to slow down, willing herself not to have to pee, she realized that she would have to renege on her promise to the humane shelter; she would have to introduce Darling to the outdoors.

She bought a red harness that took a while to put on; Darling interpreted Evan's actions as attempts to strangle her. Evan had to wear gloves. The harness went well with Darling's brown and black fur. When Evan managed to clip on the leash, she slid open the door. Darling sniffed, then stepped over the threshold.

The local flock of doves whistled in for a landing in the Jack Russell's yard and Darling ran for cover, hiding under the bush that hugged the building. Evan took Darling's instinctive behaviour as a sign that she was cautious by nature. Over the next two days, Evan untangled the leash from the bushes half a dozen times before deciding that Darling was streetwise. Darling ignored the Jack Russell's obnoxious barking and sat quietly on her side of the fence to drive him crazy, a cocky attitude that made Evan laugh. The next morning she dressed Darling in just a snap-off collar, slid the door open, and said, "Go." She knew if anything happened to Darling, it would be her fault.

After lunch Evan went outside to look and found Darling hunkered down behind a cactus over the edge of the wash. When she saw Evan, she streaked away. Evan tracked her. "Please, little one, be careful." Darling meowed at her, then crouched and wiggled her butt. Her eyes, manic slits, sized Evan up, so scary that Evan cried, "Hey! Cut that out, it's me!" The eyes refocused, the hunter vanished, and a kitty reappeared.

She phoned Eric to ask if he would like to come out for a visit. Might be nice to get away, she said.

"Unlike you," he pointed out, "I don't get school holidays." Eric worked in a land title office in busy Hamilton County, in suburban Indianapolis. He said Cathy's family was making him do the rounds of Sunday dinners. Cathy's was a big, close Catholic family. Eric was surrounded.

Joe next door fell and broke his hip. He'd had one replacement already. An ambulance pulled up to take him to the hospital. "Fallen soldier," he said to Evan as the paramedics were loading him into the ambulance. Alma moaned and started to cry and didn't cover her face with her hands. Tears poured over her open lips. "You'll be all right, woman," Joe said. "Arden will be here day after tomorrow." Arden was their son, driving down from Montana.

"You could have dinner with me," Evan said to Alma, as they watched the ambulance drive off.

Alma brightened. "I'll make my famous casserole." Evan knew the casserole was a tamale pie, made with beef and canned corn.

Arden stayed for two days. When they learned that Joe had an infection and would remain in hospital a while, Arden packed up his mother's things.

"Why are you taking her away? What about Joe?" Evan asked, seeing him throw suitcases into the back of his battered Dodge Ram.

"I have a ranch to run," he said. "And there's Mother."

Alma was wearing her favourite apron, with a print of apples and peaches. The apron was faded from the wash, but it was nicely ironed, and the lace around the edges was very white. Evan admired the apron. Alma stopped crying. "You know Joe married an older woman."

"See what I mean," said Arden. He helped his mother into the passenger seat and strapped her in. She started crying again, long sobs. "Where's Joe? Where's Joe?"

Everyone had heard stories of javelinas eating small dogs, but there wasn't any mention of them going after cats. Evan forgot to tell Darling about javelinas; she didn't give it a second thought as she tossed broccoli out the door for them and then carrots to the rabbit (to the chipmunk, really). One afternoon she entered the living room and saw Darling on the other side of the path just as the javelinas approached. It seemed wiser if Darling stayed where she was. Evan stood at the sliding door and called, "Don't move, stay there!" but Darling must have thought Evan was calling her and dashed out. The boar lowered his head and ran at her. Darling moved in zigzags toward the Jack Russell's fence and leapt in the air. The Jack Russell was barking aggressively, the javelina was ramming the wire fence, and the other javelinas were milling and squealing. Pandemonium! Evan ran for the broom just as Darling yowled, pinned between the fence and the boar's brutal snout. Evan slid open the door and ran at him, holding the broom like a spear. The boar stamped his feet and made threatening moves toward her. Evan hollered and the boar backed up, bawled, and scuttled over the edge of the wash, the squealing family following.

Evan stood huffing and puffing, the glare of the white sun off the gravel like blindness. "Darling?"

Darling had slipped to the ground, crushed, her middle oozing; just her legs flinched, bent and shocking to see. Evan couldn't touch her; Darling's teeth were bared and she growled low in her throat. The Jack Russell continued to bark. Evan looked at Joe and Alma's empty apartment, drapes closed. Joe would have known what to do. Darling's legs didn't stop twitching for a long time. Evan poked the Jack Russell with the broom, to shut it up. The ground turned red around Darling, blood mixed with sunset. A door down along the strip of apartments opened, then closed. A coyote yelped. Darling died.

Evan flew to Indianapolis to visit her brother. They sat on his porch in an older suburb and drank Jack Daniel's mixed with orange juice and Southern Comfort, a drink he'd started making when Cathy was first diagnosed.

"I think Darling was disturbed. You couldn't pet her." Evan put down her drink.

"Stop calling her that name. It was a cat. An SPCA cat."

"A humane shelter cat. Yes—but—" Then Evan shut her mouth. Cathy was a human being, a wife, her sister-in-law. Evan had wrapped Darling in a red silk shawl and buried her under the mesquite tree. The woman who worked double shifts, the owner of the Jack Russell, had offered her condolences, handed Evan an overcooked macaroni and cheese casserole, and said she had to run.

Eric swirled the liquid in his glass. He opened his mouth, poured the drink down his throat, and gargled before swallowing. "Be honest, Sis," he said. "Who do you miss most, your husband or the cat?" Someone drove up across the street and waved at Eric. Eric waved back. "Asshole," he muttered.

Evan remembered Ray, a slightly built man but strong. After he died she'd thought he had the nature of a Siamese cat, high-strung and demanding. His arms were as strong as the trunks of fibrous tropical trees. She remembered the eager, analytical talks they'd had, sitting on the bed across from each other, sometimes with tears in their eyes when what one of them said was too true. Then she remembered the bottles of alcohol tucked all over the house, and the broken crockery. She eyed her brother. "How can you be so mean?"

Eric rattled ice cubes in response and poured another drink from the pitcher at his feet.

For what felt like the longest time, her thoughts backfired in all directions as she thought about Eric's question. She missed how tight Ray could hold her, how safe he made her feel. She missed the hummingbirds that didn't come to the feeders because Joe was gone and no one filled them with syrup, and she felt sorry for the Mountain Dew birdfeeder that had broken loose in the wind and lay on the ground. She missed the daily life of worry, having her cat. "Darling," she blurted. "You."

The day after she got home, a moving van arrived and took Joe and Alma's things away. Later Evan was sitting on her sofa, the light a slurp of warm syrup over the wash, when she looked up from a new Arizona bird guide and for a moment believed she saw Alma scampering around, flapping her apron, chasing off the roadrunner.

She found Joe at Holy Family Center on St. Mary's Road, in an older section of the hospital, sharing a room with an old man who mistook Evan for someone else. "I can't find my automobile!" he shouted in an Italian-sounding accent. "I don't know where my pants are!"

"I don't know where they are, either," said Evan. "I'm sorry."

Joe reached out to shake her hand. "I need another three weeks of antibiotic treatment. Could leave tomorrow if Alma was here. Arden's got her doing tests."

"Are you going to Montana?"

Joe didn't answer. Instead, his fingers fiddled with some papers. "Aw, naw. The boy's got enough on his plate, what with Alma and that big ranch. Now here," he said, looking up, "here's the stuff I got to get to." He showed her the list of calls he needed to make—the HMO, home support care, various motels he might be able to stay in. Joe had worked as a railroad detective, and so, he told her, he knew how to get his ducks in a row. "They overmedicated me at first, and this old fool," he said, slapping his chest, "didn't know where he was and dialled 911 for help." Evan watched Joe's face change colour, flushing to a dark red of embarrassment by the time he finished relating the farcical events during his first days in hospital. He couldn't find his bill-fold, and when the credit card company phoned about unusual charges—well, of course, it was Arden in Montana with Alma. "Lost," he said. "I was just plumb lost."

"I know the feeling." She told Joe what had happened to Darling.

Joe's long face waggled as he sighed. "Javelinas will go after anything. They will eat McDonald's burger wrappers and the flowers from a Christmas cactus. They appreciate the pansies folks from Wisconsin plant for them."

The comment made her smile; winter visitors loved their pansies.

Evan examined the baffled fellow in the next bed, his face twisted in a grimace. A man of Joe's intelligence and conversational style would lose his mind if he stayed much longer. She had that spare bedroom, an extra pillow, and some blankets, and it would be easy enough to rent a bed. She could handle the IV; she had her first-aid certificate. She pictured Joe propped on her oversized sofa in the living room, watching the hummingbirds. She shifted her gaze to Joe. His eyes were the soft glistening green of a cactus after a rain. She heard his voice telling stories. She pictured the Mountain Dew bottle repaired and filled with seed. Maybe, just maybe, the Gila woodpecker would drop by for some exercise.

Miami

"At least leave me something," she'd whined, and when he did break it off, Sheryl convinced herself she was grateful for the red truck, a slightly used Blazer. Then she lost it on black ice. The truck swooped away from under her in a ripple of space and time and veered from the expected track. A new universe gaped with glory for one moment, then slammed shut the next. The truck staggered uncertainly and pitched off the road onto its side, like a wounded horse that needed to be shot. She came out of the accident bruised, one eye blackened. She came out looking like a woman who'd been beaten, or like one who'd fallen, battered by nothing but getting out of bed.

At the time of the accident, she'd bled like a stuck pig. Scalp wounds, she knew, had the capacity to startle. The ambulance guys put her in the back with the gurney. One drove and the other sat facing her, alert and watching. She'd worked in a health clinic long enough to know it wasn't because she was so lovely that he studied her; he was waiting to see if her pupils dilated, indicating shock. Her face, no doubt, was streaked with brownish, drying blood. His attention was calming. "They teach you this, don't they?" she said, and then his gaze turned wary and he reached for her wrist to check her pulse. "I'm fine," she said, "just mad as hell. The car was all I had left." Such a curious, true confession—blood and loss caused even a normally private person to spill all sorts of things. "All I had left." Her eyes stung with tears due to her voice talking in the vacuum of the ambulance and a kind man observing her.

He said, "You didn't hurt anyone. You kept control, so you didn't hit another car or smash into someone's house. I don't think you're badly hurt. A truck's only a hunk of steel."

She stared at him as though he'd missed the point, but he hadn't. Thinking about how she might have run over a kid throwing snowballs, or plowed into another vehicle, killing someone's mother, made her cry.

Bruised, she thought she looked more interesting, a person with an emotionally complex life. Her buddies at the health clinic made a case for guardian angels and loved the drama. "You didn't crash into the telephone pole," one of the nurses said. "You could have smacked it head on, been trapped inside." Because Sheryl hadn't hit anything head-on and the electrical system still worked, she'd simply scrambled through the sunroof onto the tarmac. They jabbered on about what might have transpired, instead of the rather prosaic events that did. A miracle, other staff exclaimed, wearing their pink and blue teddy bear cottons. "Huh. More like punished," Sheryl had said, thinking of the totalled vehicle. Then she figured she'd leave well enough alone. Trying for another woman's husband, even if that man was her own ex-husband, was bad karma.

She cut her curly hair short, tinted it with blond highlights. Brunette with blond streaks felt good for a day. Then she was back to where she'd started, wondering if her life mattered. She wondered if you could matter when no one loved you.

At the clinic, besides working the desk on-call, she ran a counselling group. She thought it was ironic that she, of all people, was hired to give advice to girls. She'd made a mess of things with her marriage, another mess of things with her divorce, and foolishly played around with the same man afterwards. She'd put a lot of work into him; he no longer said, "I seen." She hadn't really wanted him back, not to live with, but she was flattered by the idea that he still wanted her. Desired her sexually.

The teenaged girls in her group, from abusive situations, wore their spangled jeans tight and their tops so short their baby fat showed. They had tats and nose rings and acne and smelled like cheap vanilla. Some were farm girls who had chosen the wrong boyfriends; others needed to escape fathers or step-fathers. They thought she had it together after the accident (they respected her new hairstyle). For a while, they showed up on time, they stopped texting long enough to listen to her spiel about birth control. One of them admitted, "But I want a baby. I want someone to love me." Sheryl said, "I know the feeling." By then her bruises were fading to a tainted green.

A girlfriend talked her into a six-night "exotic" Caribbean cruise, for single baby boomers over forty. She asked a neighbour's little girl to come by every day to look after her hamster, Harry. The child was thrilled by the offer of money; it was her first real job, and Harry was so cute. Harry, a Golden, was cute. Most people Sheryl knew didn't believe someone like her would have a hamster—a hamster was a child's pet. "You don't think I'm the hamster type?" she'd ask, chewing gum with her mouth open. Sheryl had always had hamsters, and while she was married, they'd had a ferret. When she shops for groceries, Harry rides in her shirt pocket, a ball of warmth against her heart, like having a secret love.

Her seatmate on the connector between Dallas and Miami was a boy of about ten, travelling alone, stretched out on the two seats, his left arm in a sling. When she'd leaned in to claim her seat on the aisle, he'd given her the once-over, taken his feet down, pulled himself tighter toward the window. She murmured, "You'll be all right." People said she had a way with children.

She ordered a double gin and tonic. He'd been visiting a grandmother. His mother was a waitress at a resort in South Bay or North Beach, he wasn't sure. He lived at the resort, and he got to go out on big boats. Sheryl wondered what else his mother did at the resort besides waitress if she and the boy lived there. She thought about a child not sure of his whereabouts in Miami—north, south; maybe children didn't care. It was the mother who mattered to a little boy, being close to the mother. In answer to Sheryl's question about his looks, he said he was a mix of many things.

"Oh," she said. "People must think you speak Spanish."

His father was black, his mother Norwegian. His father played football and had been famous. The child himself wasn't big for his age. He had once flown first class because his father had paid for the ticket. "Oh," Sheryl said again. They would have catered to him, the light brown child in first class, they would have fed him macaroni and cheese and cut up his steak, served him extra portions of cake.

This trip in coach, he'd come all the way from his grandma's in Spokane, and because his flights were all "short haul," he'd had nothing to eat but peanuts and cookies. Grandma, the white one or the black one (Sheryl didn't ask), may not have known about short-haul flights and the fiscal fly-and-starve policy. She wondered why more fights didn't break out on planes—people with low blood sugar or, for that matter, smokers at the end of their ropes. She rummaged in her carry-on and came up with a granola bar, told him it was high in protein and had good carbs. He took it, doubtful, tore the paper off with his teeth and his free hand, gobbled it in four bites, and then thanked her.

"What happened?" She gestured toward the sling.

He shrugged, turned to the window.

She said, "I was in an accident. Totalled my car. Got out with a few bruises."

He looked at her with admiration. "Skateboard," he said.

"I loved that truck. It had sentimental value." But she hadn't deserved it, not really; she'd pressured him into buying it. She'd lied to everyone about how it had come to be hers. "I think I'm a liar. Are you a liar?"

The boy considered. His eyes were green with flecks of gold. His lashes were long and curled upwards. "Mom says to only tell white lies."

Another hour and they would land. She opened the second gin, added tonic. Every day during the affair, she'd lied by omission, she'd cracked jokes with his new wife.

"How do you define a white lie?"

"One that don't hurt," the child said and went back to fiddling with the DVD player.

The plane dipped. He turned to her. She said, "Air pocket. Just keep your seatbelt on." He was fine-boned, almost pretty, brown curls, and lips with ridged edges. Nice, she thought.

He tapped a finger on the DVD player. "Battery used up."

"They're not very good, are they?" She meant the batteries.

"This player is very good. My daddy give it to me."

"Gave it to me," Sheryl said. She'd missed her calling. If she'd been an English teacher, she could think of herself as being paid to go around correcting everyone's English. "It's my job," she would say and press the corners of her lips to bring out the dimples. She would go around correcting adults as well as children—no more "between him and I," no more "from her and myself." The child shifted in his seat. She let him sniff an empty gin mini. The airline served Tanqueray. "The good stuff," she said.

The bathroom ceiling in her motel room was slick with condensation. Outside, people splashed in a turbid pool. Fronds and tendrils of wet, unclean-seeming things unfurled everywhere. The flowers were odd and oversized, beautiful she supposed, but she would never stick her nose in to smell them, for fear of bugs or something slimy. The air smelled like it was teeming with lizards and frogs. She pulled the covers back, inspected the bed; the sheets were dubious, limp and thin. Studied the armchair before she sat down. Crossed her legs, wiggled her foot. It would be another whole day until her girlfriend arrived, and she couldn't spend the evening watching for movement in the rug.

Remembering that the cabbie had driven around and

behind the entrance to a posh hotel to deposit her where she was staying, Sheryl realized that her cheap motel and the hotel were in the same building. She found a way to get to the hotel without going outside, eventually opening a door and gliding through a magic portal from her crappy world into a nice one. The hotel's carpet was new, the wallpaper fresh; the towels on that side, she saw as she passed a house-keeping cart, were fluffy. The concierge greeted her as she stepped off the elevator. She still worked out; she was holding her shape. She felt good crossing the spacious lobby to the cocktail lounge.

The eyes of the man were the colour of honey with a dash of cinnamon. Like a tiger's eye marble, Sheryl thought. He was about her age, early to mid-forties, with a short, thick neck. His skin was burnt almond, a black man who, like the sweet little boy on the plane, was a mix of many things. She slid onto a stool and ordered a Bombay Sapphire martini to top off the drinks on the flight.

The man at the bar pulled his head back a few inches as he let her study his eyes. "Hi," she said. Far, far from home.

Well-dressed men and a few women in suits occupied the chairs at the tables. The men were watching a football game, the HD screen tilting from the wall over her left shoulder. The man with the honeyed eyes cheered at something in the game and, after a grunt to get her attention, said—still looking at the

TV—"I'm working security for the team. They had me come down early, secure the rooms."

"The team is staying here, in this hotel?"

He tossed her a scornful look. "You think you gonna get information, security-type information, out of me? Do I look like that kind of nigger?"

She was in Florida; maybe people talked that way here. She laughed as if he'd made a joke and looked to the man on her other side. This other man, in a lightweight grey suit that fit him well, was leaning against the bar eating a burger.

"That any good?" she asked.

His eyes appraised her. She was wearing a sleeveless black dress that showed some cleavage. "Not bad."

She looked through the chilled alcohol in her drink, at the cool olive on the bottom. A woman could change how a man saw her by adding a layer of heavy-duty foundation, long-lash mascara, and a simple, daring dress. Power rose in her belly, made her chortle. She thought of asking the usual questions— where he was from, line of work, how many children—but the man with the honey-and-cinnamon eyes leaned forward, square hands on the bar in front of her. "You tryin' to steal my woman?" The idea of being this stranger's woman, even for a night, felt both risky and consoling. She craved touching. Her body was jumping out of its skin for lack of touching. His skin smelled sweet, with a hint of tobacco.

The man in the suit finished his burger, pushed the plate

away, initialled the bill to his room. "You take care," he said, nodding to her, the nod an emphasis.

She had to start somewhere. They ordered burgers.

"Everybody lonely. No shame in that. Just two people," he said. He held his gaze on her, a few seconds of no escape. The waitress slid a burger across the bar in the nick of time.

"Thank you," Sheryl said.

His burger arrived, and he sent it back. "I don't want no mushrooms on this here burger. What, you crazy or something? Where's my bacon, that's what I'm asking. Just a simple order. Who are you people anyway?"

Sheryl lowered her voice. "They look Polish."

He said, "They look stupid."

"They're the new immigrants. The Slavs. The Poles. You know." She ended with "you know" because she didn't want him to feel she was thinking of slaves, *the* slaves.

She ordered a glass of white wine. He ordered Remy. "Gimme a glass of my Remy."

"Yeah, and put in lots," she laughed in the direction of the bartender, narrow cheeked, severe.

"Way to go." He bopped her shoulder with his fist, hard enough that she felt the imprint of his knuckles. She bit into her burger.

The bartender brought a tab. The man said, "You trying to hurry me out of here? Look at the price of that dinky drink. What a lousy place. Dinky drink."

To divert him from the bartender, Sheryl said, "My room has a damp ceiling. Bathroom ceiling."

"What's your room number?"

"Can't remember." She held up the wineglass so he would think drinking was the reason.

He laughed. "You come to my room. Just a little touching. You like that, don't you?"

His room, she did not doubt (based on his floral, short-sleeved shirt with embroidery on the pocket), would be as questionable as hers. Sheets worn, recycled air fragrant with eau de mildew, cigarette burns on the arm of a chair. This man would not have a room in the hotel where they were sitting. She caught the eye of the waitress, asked for her burger to be put in a takeout box. She didn't actually know what she would do next. Humidity lay like a wet blanket under the air conditioning.

She said, "It would just change my life if I did that." She longed to be a woman who made casual choices. His belly under the floral shirt looked soft, but his hands were large, exotic pink on the undersides. Indecisive, she pushed at a boundary, to see if it would budge. Would he shove her onto the bed, unzip his fly? Just two people, he'd said. That's all she ever wanted. Just two people, together. What is the deal with human beings? The urge to merge, the aversion to being alone at night.

A nineteen-yard run had the bar patrons muttering, wound up, a hint of something dangerous in the excitement. Fans in competition with each other.

"I don't discriminate," he said, eyes on the screen.

"Thank you." She finished the wine and covered the glass with her hand, intercepting the bartender.

Still watching the game, the man said, "We just have a little fun, a cuddle, some hugging and touching. You like that touching, don't you?"

She glanced shyly at the man with the special eyes, tried to imagine a cuddle. A clothes-on cuddle, his lips on her cheek, his hands rubbing her back, their thighs pressed together. She looked at the slab of half-eaten meat on a bun in a pinkish sauce, a limp lettuce leaf beside it, in the oversized Styrofoam box.

His fist hit the bar. "Bastard! Can you believe that, can you believe he just went and did that?" He turned to the room. "You over there, who you looking at? I don't like people looking where they shouldn't be looking. Hey," he said. "Hey!"

A woman accepting an invitation to a man's room was an accident waiting to happen, and, arguably, she deserved what she got. She imagined he would take a piss with the bathroom door open. He would grab her by the roots of her hair and she would see his teeth.

Judge Judy would say, "Ma'am, you went to this man's room for a cuddle? You didn't notice his volatile behaviour in the bar? How old are you, ma'am?" Shit, Sheryl thought. She let go of the Styrofoam container. Shit, she thought, and fled.

Heart of a Saint

On the day Maria Sanchez became engaged to Iosif, she told her mother that she knew, at last, why she'd waited to marry; she'd found the man she was destined to love. He'd been persecuted and tortured for his political beliefs, so he said, and lost his wife during that time, which was why he was living in Arizona. He was in his early fifties, divorced, and had no children. She liked to massage his feet. He would sit in the red leather high-back chair in their bedroom with the view of the Catalina Mountains, she facing him on the matching stool. He said she was a foot fetishist. She said she was merely a specialist, a slave to his feet because it gave him pleasure, and pleasure was what she wanted him to have.

The day she turned thirty-four, he sent yellow roses to her office in the resort where she worked in accounting. By that time, they'd been married a year. For dinner he prepared steak au poivre. Three candles in silver holders flickered on the table between them. Cognac and cream coated her lips. She said, "My love, please give us a child." He set his cutlery down, lowered his gaze. He was balding just at the crown. When he raised his eyes to hers, they swam with tears. He then told her the first lie: "I didn't want to lose you. But—you understand—I can't father children." The words *imprisonment* and *torture* moved through the ether between them. She shuddered. "I am so sorry to have brought it up."

Later that week Maria drove to her mother's house in an older, elegant section of Tucson, on a street lined with palm trees. In her mother's living room, which smelled of lavender and anise, Maria stroked the fine lace antimacassars on the arms of a chair, the lace an old-fashioned touch that contrasted nicely with the flat-screen television on the wall, before she made her announcement: "Mama, there will be no grandchildren." The grandfather clock chimed the quarter-hour.

Theresa Sanchez, who was fair-skinned and patrician, said, "I am not surprised."

Maria sighed. "Mama, I'm falling into one of the traps you always set for me, but here I go. Why are you not surprised?"

"Iosif is Gestapo."

"Ay, Mama. He is not Mexican, he will never be Mexican."
Theresa Sanchez did not trust him, she'd told her daughter,
and therefore, to her, he was "Gestapo." Her houses and
property would go to her daughter, but not to her daughter's
husband.

Her mother's bracelets jangled as she set the small glass of
sherry on the mesquite hardwood table beside her. "I always
wanted a boy."

Maria smiled—this gambit, too, was familiar. She came
forward, took her mother's soft hands between her two palms,
and knelt at her feet. "I also wanted a boy." In this way Maria
maintained the balance between them.

Her mother laughed. "I can't shake you, can I?" She spoke
in Spanish, referring to a popular song. She touched her lips
to Maria's hands and Maria laughed and went back to where
she'd been sitting. Her mother was full of surprises—now,
Mexican pop songs. Maria watched the doves fluttering on the
patio behind the open blinds. Small birds, tiny yellow verdins
and goldfinches, took turns ruffling their feathers in the three-
tiered fountain that looked like a wedding cake.

Her mother rolled her eyes heavenward, lifted the cross
from her neck, and kissed it. "I apologize. You are my one and
only child, and for you I am grateful."

Maria felt a shiver up her back. "Mama," she said. "Stop
being nice. It's upsetting."

"You will have a boy, a boy will come to you."

"Mama, we would need a miracle."

"Milagros vivos." Miracles live.

Theresa Sanchez died of a brain aneurysm. Maria inherited the house in Tucson and her mother's properties in Yuma, on the other side of the state. Maria arranged for the funeral mass, held at the Mission San Xavier del Bac—the White Dove of the Desert—on the Tohono O'odham reservation south of Tucson. The restoration of the eighteenth-century mission—an eclectic mix of Moorish, Byzantine, Mexican, and Indian influences—had been Theresa's passion; when she was able, she had volunteered every week. Mission San Xavier del Bac was famous among the religious for the carved figure of Saint Francis Xavier, said to bring answers to prayers, that lay under a yellow cotton coverlet on a platform in an alcove. Notes, cards, photographs, and Milagros, religious charms, were pinned to the fabric—tiny photos of children, Milagros of arms and legs, a horse, a foot, and a heart, things that had been found or healed.

After the mass and the receiving line, Maria stayed to touch the bosom of the saint and pray for intercession for her mother's soul. She reached out her hand and placed it on the saint's chest among the treasures. She could feel tingling as energy from his heart lifted hers. Her mind opened and a light entered—a mysterious and breathtaking light—her mother, blessing her.

Iosif waited outside.

The following Monday Maria found a letter on the hall table. It lay hidden under a copy of the *Arizona Daily Sun* and a *Harper's*. She saw Iosif's name on the front but opened it because the handwriting was childish, the letters rounded. She assumed it was from one of her foster children. Mail back and forth was slow—she'd told "her children" about her wedding, and for an eleven-year-old girl in Africa or Peru to write "Joseph" on the envelope might be childish teasing. She smiled and opened the crumpled note. It read: *I am sick. I have made many mistakes in my life. I need your help Papa. Sephara.*

Papa? She thought the office that handled her foster children had made a mistake. She flipped the envelope over. Joseph. It was addressed to Joseph Cizardi. The name spelled differently than she knew it.

She looked at the note again. There was an e-mail address at the bottom.

She drove to the resort and walked across the path, past hummingbirds tissing in the shrubs of desert honeysuckle, and into her office. She shut the door. Iosif had told her practically nothing of his past. "Please," he would say. "I've had enough—" *Torture.* The word lay always between them. In empathy her heart rose; her love made her quiver. He would detect her vulnerability, her desire, and he would sweep her into bed, undress her, layer by layer until she was shivering with anticipation, and then undress himself. Slow and tantalizing, he would wrap his arms and legs around hers, penetrate her carefully, hold her until they both could hardly stand it and would cry out together.

Iosif was only her third lover. The first was careless and bit her lips, and they occasionally bled. Then she'd let herself become engaged to a man uninterested in sex. He invariably couldn't come, and his hands were clammy. Afterwards, Maria volunteered at the hospital in the maternity ward, adopted foster children in three countries, and had decided sex was overrated until Iosif touched her.

She swirled the chair to the computer screen and typed a simple, truthful response to the note addressed to "Papa." She signed it: "Maria, Iosif's third wife."

She pressed Send. Her chair squeaked as she sat back, as it always did. It started to rain, the afternoon monsoon. Maria thought: A second wife is a rebound. A third wife is a stranger.

Iosif read the note. He told Maria that the writer wasn't his biological daughter; she was a stepchild. This was his second lie, Maria would discover. Iosif said the girl had been wild—she'd had mononucleosis more than once, he said, from her careless sleeping around.

"How long have you been her father?"

"I was never her father."

"How long were you married to Sephara's mother?"

Iosif said, "It is in the past."

Maria received an e-mail answer, typed at a library in Albuquerque. Sephara was twenty-seven. She hadn't lived a careful life. She had been diagnosed with Hodgkin's lymphoma. She said it was her fault. She asked her father's forgiveness.

Maria wrote: "Hodgkin's lymphoma isn't your fault."

Around then, Iosif and a colleague from the university, a fellow enthusiast of antique musical instruments, made plans to attend a three-day conference in Phoenix. Maria made her own plans for her first trip to Albuquerque. She stayed at a good hotel downtown. She felt uncertain of herself, as though her spirit was someone else's—someone unpredictable, a woman who would deceive her husband for the truth.

She touched the cross she wore at her throat when the taxi stopped at Sephara's address. The taxi driver had already told her it was a bad neighbourhood. "Pueblo people," he said, watching her, trusting that Maria, in her business clothes and shoes, was not Native. Maria opened the door, heard rap music, and picked her way around broken beer bottles. The taxi waited while Maria rang the buzzer. A young woman appeared, wearing grey sweatpants and a T-shirt. The young woman was the spitting image of her father, Maria's own Iosif. Behind her tumbled a child.

Sephara said, "I couldn't tell you about my son. I was ashamed." She introduced her three-year-old, Jorge. Jorge had a mop of black hair. He had fine bones and was the colour of frothy Mexican chocolate. He had a space between his teeth, laughing lips, and the light-hearted attitude of a pixie.

Maria cited issues with tenants in Yuma as her excuse to Iosif for her three-day weekends. She went back and forth to Albuquerque. Over lunch at a McDonald's, Maria learned that Sephara's mother had become ill with breast cancer and died when Sephara was fifteen, and that her father, disapproving of her tattoos and her lifestyle, left her when he moved to Los Angeles to marry again. Staying in an abandoned building with friends her age, she quit school, worked as a waitress. Later she went back to night school to finish her degree and, instead, became pregnant.

During another visit, Maria learned that the father of Jorge was probably Mexican, from a good family that wouldn't acknowledge a child out of wedlock. Then Sephara lowered her head and confessed that she did not know for sure.

On her third visit, Maria rented a car, and she and Sephara and Jorge drove to the suburbs to a big grocery store with fresh vegetables and good-quality meat. Coming out of the store, pushing the cart loaded with good food, Maria glanced in the grocery store window. "Stop, look," she said to them. "Take my hand." Maria, Sephara, and Jorge lined up and examined themselves. They looked related. The child had Maria's unruly, curly hair. He had his grandfather's eyes.

Sephara needed radiation treatments. Maria flew them back with her to Tucson and put them up in her mother's house, with some trepidation. A young woman who had lived on her own in squalor might turn her mother's beautiful home into a mess, but Sephara was respectful and kept it clean and shiny. She was a good cook. The house was close enough to the university, where she went for radiation treatments. Hodgkin's lymphoma was treatable and her prognosis was good. Maria arranged for Jorge to begin preschool in the neighbourhood.

She bided her time. On the anniversary of her mother's passing, in Iosif's big house with the view of the Catalina Mountains, she said to her husband, "I expect a miracle today." She was hosting a remembrance for her mother at Mission San Xavier del Bac, and many volunteers, as well as Theresa Sanchez's friends, would be in attendance. Sephara and a friend of Maria's would be there also, with Jorge, to introduce the child to his grandfather. Maria felt very hopeful, because on her side she had two saints—her mother and Saint Francis—against one man, his soul imperilled by deception.

At the mission standing in line at the saint's image, Maria asked that Iosif be with her. "Please," she said. "For me." When it was their turn to touch the carved wooden image, Maria placed Iosif's soft hand on the heart of the saint. "Why didn't you contact your daughter?"

"I never had a daughter. It is a great sorrow."

Maria's smile faltered. The third lie. They moved quickly

out of the line and moved without touching each other from the church. Outside the sky was the lilac blue of the Sonoran desert on a winter afternoon. Against it, Iosif's forehead looked sunburned.

"Please. She was wayward," he said. "Nothing more," he said.

Maria's love took flight at his words.

She tilted her neck to gaze at the ornate wooden doors of the church and its two white domes, and the doves flying overhead. She turned again and noted a pilgrim climbing the hill to a shrine. Near the top she saw a palm tree, and behind it, in the glittering rays of the sun, she saw her mother.

Maria turned her body again, this time toward the parking lot. She spotted Jorge waving from the back window of the car. Sephara, in the passenger seat, waited for Maria's signal.

Maria stared at the lids of her husband's downcast eyes. She lowered herself to catch his gaze, tilted her head to search for the light, saw darkness.

His soul was lost, unrepentant; she had nothing more to say to him. She stepped back and walked way, leaving him standing where he was. If his eyes turned to follow her, she did not feel them on her back. Within her mother's radiance, she strode toward Sephara and the little Jorge, laughing with joy to see her, the two a testament to her mother's belief that without a doubt, *sin duda*, miracles live.

Open to Interpretation

The day started with Barb forgetting to connect the sway bar between the Explorer and the travel trailer. Along the way, she would be arrested and then released from a holding cell.

Barb had set off early, leaving a woodsy little campsite by a river near a train track. The train roared by all night and shook the camper. She couldn't wait to get out of there. On the highway north of Coeur d'Alene, as the road descended, the travel trailer began to dance and Barb muttered, "Damn lot of wind out there." Other drivers slowed and changed lanes. Seeing them falling back and scattering away reminded her of the missing sway bar. "Good Christ!" Barb hollered. "Are you a fucking idiot?"

Apparently she was. Through the rear-view, Barb saw the travel trailer wobbling from one wheel to the other. Were she to slam on the brakes, it would torque off the hitch. Painfully slowly, she applied the brakes until the trailer was under control. The shoulder was narrow where she managed to pull off the highway, a flimsy guardrail between her and the abyss on one side and speeding traffic on the other. Drivers honked. "Piss off!" Barb yelled.

That evening she would be in a stranger's house, in the kitchen of a defunct pig farm in northern Idaho, sipping Jack Daniel's and taking bites of Alice Cavender's homemade, hot-out-of-the-oven chocolate chip cookies. Barb would choose to stop at Cavender's Pigs and RV Storage (just in time for Alice, as it turned out) only because her ten-year-old grandson, Rodney, collected ceramic pigs. Cavender's Pigs had seemed like a destiny, as she was out wandering Idaho roads looking for a place to store her camper instead of home by the fire in British Columbia. Because, well, because earlier she had been arrested at the border.

"Wait."

Barb was heading back to the Explorer after using the border station washroom. Snow fluttered around the Canadian customs officer, a kid with a blaze of red on his cheeks, standing between her and the Explorer.

"Why didn't you claim the trailer?" he asked.

"What?"

"The trailer," he said.

"You just waved me through."

"The licence plate."

Barb had parked so the plate was visible from the station, hadn't given it a thought. The plate shouted ARIZONA. She squinted to give the impression she was trying to see better and marvelled over it as though she had never laid eyes on it before, then swiveled her gaze back to the officer. "Wow, who knew? The trailer isn't mine, technically."

The uniformed young man with his curly blond hair looked like an older version of Rodney. For his birthday, she had brought Rodney a set of porcelain salt-and-pepper shakers on her visit to the family in Flagstaff, Arizona. She said the collection would be worth money someday. Louis, Rodney's fourteen-year-old brother, had scoffed. "Hey, little bro, there's more money in music than pigs." Louis's original plot (when he was about seven) was to take over the world and get everyone's money, but that plan had evolved to becoming a world-famous DJ, preferably at a club, so he could have a fan base.

Barb opened her mouth to tell this amusing little story to the officer, but the young man's gaze remained intense. He was like a hunting dog at point. Come to think of it, he would not be interested in the story. She said, "The trailer is my brother's.

His tow vehicle gave up the ghost. I'm doing him a favour." The blots of colour on the young officer's cheeks became brighter. He didn't step aside or wish her a good day. She played with versions of a theme, creating a friable groundwork, searching for the answer that would let her slip through the cracks. "My brother's going to fly to Spokane, rent a car."

Hearing herself talking and him not budging or answering, Barb realized that bad news was on the way. She wanted to change her mind, turn around, skip the border crossing, and announce she'd forgotten to visit a friend in Idaho. And leave. But like a lot of things in life, there was no turning back. He held out his hand. "Keys, ma'am." She dug the keys out of her jeans pocket and placed them in his palm. He unlocked the car door and gestured for her to open the glove compartment.

She riffled through papers until she found the Arizona registration from the glove box, knowing exactly what it said—the name of the owner, the name of the lienholder. It looked like her brother owned the camper, but it was actually hers, as lienholder; the registration was waffly at best. The plan she and her brother had hatched had to do with vehicles purchased in the States that the provincial government would impose taxes on when the vehicle was brought into Canada.

"Come with me."

People camping a night here, a week there, don't care about accuracy or truth; it was possible, just possible that lately Barb had fallen out of reality and into lying. She made up things about herself and her life. Why not? No one asked questions. In the end, all conversations among travellers on the road came down to God's will, unpredictable weather, and the vagaries of their adult children.

At the candy machine outside the double doors of the customs building, she stopped. "Do you mind? I'm starving." She traded the officer two US dollars for a toonie, and he murmured that she had lost a bit on the transaction. His honesty made her think she might be all right. Or would she? Some comeuppance felt at hand, for all her rash behaviours, her easy lies. At the counter she gnawed hunks of the Snickers bar while he asked more questions about ownership, and busily filled out forms.

"My brother wants to come up to fish," Barb said. More lies, a stuck record.

She felt the excitement of the listening staff.

Ten bottles of good California wine, unclaimed, concealed in the camper, were about to go down the drain, the most expensive pee stop in her history.

A female officer in tight pants and boots appeared at her side. "Come with me."

She trundled along a corridor, with Barb following. The officer opened a cell, ushered her in.

"My, they're taking wine seriously these days."

The cell door clicked shut, locked. There was one high window, a cedar bough visible through it. Along the wall opposite was a narrow counter with a phone on it. The floor was concrete. Barb sat on the slats that made a narrow bench and began to shake as though she was freezing.

Outside, car doors opened and closed, trucks lumbered by.

Hadn't she herself driven slowly, gratefully, past some poor bastard in the midst of a car search, his stuff all over the ground while he stood by looking ashamed or angry or guilty—oh, everyone is guilty of something. Barb sat on that slat bench and imagined the gratified, relieved glances of her fellow citizens, safely through the border and on their way home, and she wondered, as well, if her neighbours would recognize the car and know who it was being held, suddenly a criminal.

Eager for a search, half the station would be out there, pawing through her things—gloved hands unscrewing jars of cream, handling the silverware, rummaging through her underwear, eyes reading scraps of writing, noses sniffing cooking herbs. It was a travesty to imagine her little life—her bed sheets, clothing, laundry, shampoos, towels, pots, and pans—spread on the ground for everyone crossing the border to see. Everything exposed.

She could conjure a story, a realistic but simple story about the Smith & Wesson they were going to find: she bought the pistol at a gun show, or a relative loaned it to her, or a man, a friend, gave it to her. Those were possibilities about the gun's provenance. She was a woman travelling alone. Any American would encourage her to carry self-protection, and, in fact, had. But a disturbing thought tickled the surface. What they believed, or didn't believe, didn't count. Wouldn't count. Facts complicated things—the truth mattered less than the fact the gun had crossed a line in the soil.

"Do you need to use the washroom?"

"What?" Barb pulled her jacket from her face, sat up. Blinked at the overhead light.

"It's been two hours," the female officer said.

In the washroom the officer said, "I'm sorry about the mirrors." Barb drank some water and peed, and her bottom—she could see it too—her own little old baggy butt was observed through mirrors. They did have mirrors in jail washrooms; Barb made a note to tell the boys.

A little later, the officer said, "You have a lot of things in the trailer, but the good news for you is that the gun was stuffed in your T-shirt basket by the bed instead of up front in the cab, within reach."

The door locked. Barb looked at the cedar bough, snow making little piles, building, falling through. She said, "Gun? What gun?"

"You're going to need a lawyer." The officer handed her a list and told her to use the phone in the cell. She wondered if the line was bugged. She selected a name from the list and punched in the numbers. A lawyer in Vancouver answered the phone himself. He sounded young too, another kid. He asked her for the facts, and, just as she was starting to explain things, he said, "Stop. Look. I don't get paid for this." Again she was just getting a new story together when he interrupted: "You're a babbler." She tried to object. He raised his voice: "If you say one more word, I'm hanging up." Then he added, "Are you stupid? Are you an idiot? You are in real trouble. Keep your mouth shut." This last he shouted.

A tall, dark-haired man in jeans arrived outside her cell door and asked if he could come in. "Okay." She agreed as though she had a say in the matter. He brought a bottle of water for her. This thoughtfulness was touching, but she supposed that getting on her good side was his job.

He was muscular and wore a black T-shirt that read, RCMP. Handcuffs dangled from his belt.

He set the water on the floor and then eased onto the bench and sat so close that his shoulder touched hers. "Sorry for the wait. I'm Mike. I was up by Invermere." He handed over his card. The card read: UNDERCOVER.

"How can you be undercover if your name is on this card?"

His brown eyes were soft. "You must be tired and upset."

You bet she was upset. Tears welled up and dripped onto her jeans.

"Sorry about the wine. A little grass might have been understandable."

She thought the mention of the grass was a trap.

"But . . . a gun?"

She shrugged and stayed silent. Man, she didn't know anything, wouldn't say anything, she regretted the whole pitiful day, and being identified as a babbler cut to the quick. Maybe, just maybe, to avoid lying Barb would have to keep her mouth shut.

There was a long drive to a police station for fingerprinting.

Back at the border she had a choice: they would compound the trailer and she could continue home without it, or she could go back with it across the line.

The back seat and storage area of her car looked like it had been the victim of a robbery; God knew what the camper would look like inside. It was easier to drive than think. At two in the afternoon she turned back to Idaho.

In a border town, she spotted a phone outside a Safeway.

Kids in camouflage skated past her as she pressed the numbers. She imagined herself at home, sorting through mail, when her brother in Arizona answered.

"Sure, I'll look up criminal lawyers—barristers, whatever they call them up there. Give me a call tomorrow."

Anxiety was making her scalp itch. "Call before noon. Please."

"You sound upset. Get some rest."

She wasn't going to cry now.

"Sis, I'm on it."

Something not good and not formed by her own imagination—hello, real world—had found her.

Where to leave the camper?

It turned out that in northern Idaho there were plenty of RV and camper storage facilities, mostly located on farms no longer farms. Storing motor homes and fifth-wheelers for Canadians was a whole sideline business, a quiet cross-border agreement that, unlike free trade, Barb thought, benefitted both parties. Too bad she hadn't known about this enterprise before.

The road ambled next to a river. She drove past stored RVs with US plates, owned, no doubt, by fellow Canadians not wanting to pay those pesky taxes. Barb came to an old wooden barn with faded words painted in curly letters: CAVENDER'S PIGS, FAMILY OWNED SINCE 1898. On a new steel structure she read: CLEAN, SAFE RV STORAGE.

Thinking of Rodney, she turned in and parked by the sheds. She opened the camper door for the first time and shut it again.

Walking across the yard, she heard a strangled cry. She hurried onto the porch and looked through the screen door. She pulled the door open and strode in, to see a woman about her age in front of the fireplace, hands up over her head. A strapping boy, around fifteen, was pointing a BB gun at her.

The boy's worldly cover was familiar to Barb—instead of a ring in his lip, like Louis, this boy had a ring in his ear. His face was red, as though he'd been crying or shouting. He used the back of his free hand to rub bubbles of mucous off his face and then swung the gun in Barb's direction.

"Oh, for God's sake, put that down," she said. "I've just about had it for one day."

Customs had emptied the cupboards, jumbled all her clothes, and yanked sheets off the bed. Her herbs and spices were dumped in the sink. The bathroom's contents—cosmetics and shampoo and everything private and personal—had been tossed on the floor. She could hardly stand to think about it—*she* was the one who stopped in the first place. And now here was this preposterous situation.

"I am a certified criminal and that is the truth," she said. "I have a record. Do you see these dark marks on my fingers? Those are from being fingerprinted."

The scowl on the boy's face deepened. "Who are you?"

"Better you don't know." She tapped her leg. A big-screen TV dominated the living room, and this boy would figure "hidden weapon." The BB gun wavered. Barb crossed the room, clapped her hand around the barrel. The kid let go of it and slammed out the back door.

"Tuck it under the sofa for now," said the woman, heading for the kitchen. Barb overheard her on the phone asking a neighbour to talk to the boy.

After introductions, Alice Cavender gathered a mixing bowl, chocolate chips, butter, and flour, while Barb sat at the maple kitchen table. "He's worried, like we all are. He wants to hold a dance here—a rave, they call it. He says they'll pay us. A rave here, right here on our farm. This is a pig farm."

The sun shone on the dish drainer. Alice beat the butter with a hand mixer and when the noise stopped, she said, "He misses his Grandpa Henry. I do too." She glanced at Barb. "Henry always liked a sip midday, and you look like you could use one yourself." She poured a whiskey into a crystal glass for Barb, then added a dollop to her own coffee cup. "Truth is, last pig went on Thursday."

"There's more money in music than pigs, so I've been told." Barb studied the amber liquid in the glass and started her story, about the grandsons and the wine. It was a rambling story, even to Barb's ear.

"High taxes up there, I hear," Alice finally said.

The drink, and the hospitality of a stranger, had loosened her tongue, but Barb could not admit everything; it was too embarrassing—the jail cell, the irrevocability of being locked up, the ugly finality to the personal story she'd been weaving as she drove and camped, saw vistas and sunsets, visited family, laughed with strangers, made up stories. She wiped her cheeks.

"Now, now," soothed Alice, dropping dough onto a cookie sheet. "You might be a liar, but your timing was good. Some things seem predetermined to happen. You showing up when you did."

A wind rustled the leaves outside. "What will you do with the BB gun?"

Alice frowned. "Do with it? You think that's the only gun in the house?"

Strange how matter-of-fact Americans were about guns. Americans had encouraged her to carry a gun in the first place.

Alice said, "We live in the country." As though that would be reason enough.

"Oh." The explanation sounded rational in Idaho but didn't make sense across the border.

"My dear, he didn't mean any harm. His parents were in the military, both killed in Iraq. Didn't used to take women for combat duty. This is my daughter's third anniversary. Killed fighting for her country. It's not what we raised her for, but Henry and I were both proud of her." The cookies slid into the oven.

Barb sipped her drink. "I'm sorry about your daughter."

"And sorry about the war too, I take it, you being from Canada who didn't go."

The pig salt-and-pepper shakers on the white doily were

both pink and had smiles. Barb wondered if Louis and Rodney had such easy access to guns. Would her son-in-law allow it in Flagstaff?

"You weren't worried?"

"Naturally I was worried. You don't like to see a boy that upset. He had his reasons." Alice opened the oven to check on the cookies, turned and peered at Barb over the rims of her glasses. "They fingerprint you just for wine?"

Reality twisted like a knife in the heart and it was painful. Barb stumbled through the story of the gun.

"Oh, isn't that ridiculous," Alice Cavender snorted. "To treat you like that, as though you were a common criminal. As though a woman your age would be a danger to anyone." She removed the cookies from the oven, slipped them loose with a spatula. "Here now."

The kitchen smelled sweet and homey. Barb reached for a cookie, let it warm her palms. When she had entered the house, she'd witnessed a boy boiling with rage and nearly out of control. Mall shootings, theatre shootings—it was a criminal act to bring a handgun into Canada. That was a fact. She should have known better. She hadn't even known where to keep it—in sight or out of sight, the gun was always on her mind. Barb said, "Actually, I'm glad they found it."

Alice shook her head "To each his own. You can camp here tonight, there's an empty hay shed, nice and clean, where you can sort through your things, if you like."

"Thank you." Barb sighed with relief. One short walk to her bed, one short walk to her home on the road.

Alice lifted her apron over her head, hung it on a hook. She came back to the table, the Jack Daniel's in hand. "Canadians," she said, in her tone something both sorrowful and accepting, as she poured another shot for each of them.

Delilah

If Sheila's companion, Delilah, were a colour, she would be orange. A dusky orange that sends out occasional flares, but mostly the colour of kindling burnt to embers. Sheila construes that Delilah is this colour partly by what she says, but also by the way she speaks, with the modern artifice many women in broadcasting have, front teeth biting off words, lips softly chewing them. Sheila notices these women on TV and listens to them on the radio; the way they speak seems contrived and unnatural. She doesn't know about Delilah's tongue or lips or what she looks like. Delilah speaks to her on 94.9 MIX FM, beginning at 9:00 PM. Delilah is the voice of lovelorn southeast Arizona.

In Sheila's experience, neighbours in Arizona aren't so much visited as observed. If seen at all. She's more likely to see a feral cat skulking about than a human taking a stroll. Even here, in what calls itself a village, people drive cars from one end to the other, and except for the people who work in the retail shops, everyone else seems to have gone on holiday. You never see anyone sitting in gardens or on patios. You seldom hear a thing. Twice a day the train goes by, and the birds, cactus wrens and quail, carry on conversations among themselves.

Thank goodness for her only real neighbours, the young couple from Michigan, Amanda and Vincent, with their baby, Josephine, who live across the road. They built their adobe house on land inherited from a travelling grandparent. Josephine has a mop of very black hair that the blondish father jokes about. Sheila likes to imagine why; she's being preposterous, of course, but there are so many sweet-faced Mexican boys around here.

From her balcony, Sheila sees their window aglow with candlelight. The candlelight in the golden room reminds Sheila of when she helped Amanda sort through paint chips to create just that lovely effect. She was part of the house project since its inception—offered advice on window placement and flooring and watched over tools left in the yard by workers. Consequently, her neighbours' house—real adobe, a Southwest tradition—is a pleasure that feels like her own.

Yet there's that eucalyptus tree, far too tall for a house that lies so low to the ground. The couple built around the tree, to save it, but Sheila objects to it. From her second-floor balcony, looking across the dirt road from her apartment above a jewellery shop —chunks of turquoise and the work of Navaho silversmiths— the tree spoils her view of the mountains to the east.

Amanda and Vincent's most recent concern was the impending visit of an uncle from England. After visiting friends in San Diego, he would be hopping over to Tucson on a commuter flight. The uncle, a bachelor, was a concierge at a posh English hotel. Sheila looked up the hotel online. Nice, not showy, established, discreet. Due to Josephine, he couldn't stay with them; he'd have been driven mad by the fretful crying and early dawns.

"Of course your uncle can stay at my place," she'd said, handing them a jar of her homemade jalapeno jelly. "What's his name?"

Sheila's apartment, a two-bedroom, made it easy for her to move the unopened boxes—a testament to her inability to commit to a place—from her room to the spare bedroom. When that was done, she drove into Tucson and bought a cot and some sheets for it. The cot-sized sheets weren't very nice sheets; she found them at Ross, and the colour of the top and bottom didn't quite match. But it wouldn't matter. She would be in the spare bedroom on the cot, and he, the English bachelor named Earl, would have the master bedroom with its expensive, queen-sized bed, solid mesquite. It had been outrageous to spend so much on a bed, but she'd thought that she would find a new man, a new life. Daunting to realize how hopeful she'd been. The cot, now that she had it, seemed sensible.

She'd driven into Tucson to meet Earl at the airport, taking the I-19 to the Valencia cut-off. She was picking him up because Amanda and Vincent were occupied by baby worries—a little diarrhea that was soon corrected. And Sheila was willing. She had recognized Earl right away, based on advance description. He was a short man, the sturdy type Sheila liked, squarely built and nearly bald. She could imagine him in a kilt; his legs were bandy and strong. She wore the emerald green silk scarf that went nicely with her curly red hair. They shook hands in the arrivals level and waited at the luggage carousel, each intent on spotting his checked bag. From the freeway, as they drove past the Indian reservation, he admired the San Xavier mission.

In her living room—she thought it best if he brought his things inside before going over to spend time with Amanda and Vincent—Earl presented her with two slim cans of Marks & Spencer gin and tonic. "I wouldn't normally bring such a wee token for my host or hostess," he said, "but this is so good—and not available here, I gather—and they told me you're fond of G&Ts. As I am myself."

At that moment she was out of Gordon's gin—she saw herself flying to Safeway to get a big bottle even as she blushed. In Australia, a sheila refers to a girl or young woman, and while Sheila was neither—she was in her fifties, her prime—she still flushed when flustered.

"It's delightful of you." She reached for his hand. He was confused by the gesture—she hadn't known what she was thinking, either, so they shook hands again before she ducked onto the balcony. From there she showed him how to get to his nephew's house. She pointed out the entrance, just beyond the lowest branch of the too-tall eucalyptus.

Later, watching the candlelight in her neighbours' window, she sits with her Gordon's and Schweppes tonic (more British, she thinks, than Canada Dry), tucked farther back on her balcony than usual so she can't be seen. A full moon is just rising over the flat-topped buildings to the east and shines through the branches of the eucalyptus, its leaves rattling in the wind. It has been dry; no rain for too long. The radio in the room behind her is turned low, to Delilah's show. A girl with a sweet voice, a young mother with a live-in boyfriend, phones Delilah and says, "I just love him with everything I am."

Though Sheila can't say she's actually experienced loving someone with everything she is, she's sure she would know were it to happen.

Delilah deftly moves in on the sweet girl like a coyote to a kill. "You're grateful because he's living with you? Has he asked you to marry him? He's living with you and not willing to make the commitment to you and your two-year-old daughter? What kind of example do you think this is for your little girl? She takes him into her heart and life with no guarantee he'll always be there for her?" The sweet-voiced mother collapses in tears. She hadn't thought about her boyfriend in that way before.

Now Delilah softens and murmurs to the girl, "Sometimes we don't always make good choices," and then plays "My Prayer" by The Platters. The tender old song causes Sheila's eyes to smart.

She can't help but notice that Amanda and Vincent seem to be having a party. Some people she recognizes—gallery and restaurant owners—arrive by foot. She sips her drink and listens to the wind and the rattle of the eucalyptus leaves as the moon climbs. Someone strums a guitar.

She puts down her G&T to photograph the moon, a long exposure. She's recently bought a tripod for her digital camera and is thinking of joining a local photography group.

There is nothing more beautiful than an Arizona sky, she'd e-mailed friends back in Portland, where she used to live. She made the sky the reason she'd stayed, made the sky worth all the disappointments. She'd joined a walking group that met early every Sunday and went for big breakfasts afterwards. They often chose the Longhorn Café at the Arivaca junction, where you could order the most exotic thing—chilaquiles, eggs scrambled with green chiles and fried tortillas—so scrumptious, they were practically indecent—all that grease! Sometimes the group went south, for huevos rancheros at a Mexican café that smelled like simmering pork. She'd joined a book club at the library because there were widowers around, or so her bridge group told her, all of them married, except for the happy solo player. Then she'd joined the country club to learn to golf—men were golfers in Arizona—but that hadn't worked out; she'd damaged her rotator cuff.

She's still sitting, watching, when she sees Earl leave the neighbours' and make his way back to her. She has the Gordon's in the freezer but wonders if she's made a mistake; being British he might prefer his drink tepid. She opens the door before he has a chance to knock, her drink in hand. "Come sit on the balcony," she says. "It's windy out, but rather pretty. Quite a wonderful moon. Would you care to join me for a G&T?"

He wouldn't; he's had beer and a Caesar salad with too much garlic. He explains the way a Caesar salad should be made—slivered egg, shaved Parmesan, freshly baked croutons. Earl uses his hands as he talks, describing the sort of garlic a good chef uses. He tells her the chef in his hotel is top-notch. She admits to loving perfection in food. He sits a few moments in silence and then checks his watch. He says, "Travel tires one, even short-haul flights, indeed it does. I wish you good night."

On the cot, Sheila wears earphones to listen to the radio so as not to disturb her guest. Delilah is married for the second time and believes in God. She has a little boy now and a loving husband. She says, "God bless you" when people are in dire straits and she says, "Let's pray" when things are worse than dire. Every night, Delilah speaks comforting words. It's Sheila's second spring in this particular desert, the fulsome season preceding godawful heat and monsoons, a time of grace, the mammals pregnant or nursing, babies birthed; eggs hatched, chicks feeding. There's tranquility in the Sonoran desert, a sense of plenty. But Delilah knows her audience isn't living a natural, seasonal cycle. Tonight she says a variation of her usual: "Some of you are sad over a lost love, someone you thought would be with you forever, and I'm here to help you, ease your hearts, make your evening just a little brighter. Call me with your stories and let me play something special for you and the person you're thinking of." Around eleven, heading toward midnight, Delilah reminds her audience to love someone tonight.

Sheila turns off the radio and places the earphones on the table. She settles in. Wonders if he snores.

In the morning her guest emerges from the bedroom wearing a satin dressing gown and carrying his own shampoo. "Very comfortable bed," he says. "Quite good of you to let me use it."

"My pleasure." She's making coffee, which he doesn't drink, but tea would be welcome.

"I need no breakfast, thank you. We're going out and then will carry on, spending the day in wine country. Though it is hard to believe that grapes grow in the desert."

Sheila says, "Oh, yes, they do! Around Elgin and Sonoita there are beautiful wineries. Lovely area! I just so enjoy a day in the high desert."

The phone rings. Sheila flutters her fingers at her guest. "Excuse me."

The call is from Amanda. "Hey. Hi. If you'd like to meet us for breakfast, that would be great. You'll have to bring your own car. The Nissan's so small, what with the car seat . . ."

Sheila gives the words a moment.

Amanda says, "We're going to that place near the border that makes the fabulous huevos rancheros. The place you like so much. Then we'll play it by ear, maybe take Earl for a drive."

Sheila thinks about the party the night before. Thinks about her comment just now to Earl about a day in the high desert. Thinks about how foolish she is. She hesitates, glances at the back of the man in his dressing gown as he shuts the bathroom door, and turns toward the phone. She's effusive with her thanks for the invitation—"Jam-packed day planned," she says, and, gushing, declines.

Driving that night down through Yuma and into the Laguna Mountains on a spontaneous visit to San Diego—she will keep driving west until the road runs out—she discovers there's more to Delilah than she knew. In fact, there is another Delilah entirely. This woman's voice is a little huskier. This new Delilah speaks the same words, and she, too, wants to help. This Delilah says, "I know you're a little tired, and I know you've had a long day today, and that's why I'm here."

Sheila is more than a little tired. She left a key in an envelope with Earl's name on it, on the welcome mat, and has been driving for nine hours, dealing with bouts of weeping along the way. It was idiotic to set out at the time of day she did, but she couldn't stand the sight of her neighbours' empty house and the silence in her own. Now she's tearing along in the dark at seventy miles an hour on a deserted highway, clinging to the murmuring predictability of Delilah and the emotional wrench of desolation that she expects will well up at the next song. Delilah, she thinks, is as addictive as Facebook and just about as productive. Sheila's heart is not eased when she listens to Delilah: the romantic dirges she plays make Sheila want to send out flares—"Over here! Over here!" Dance like crazy or sink into simplistic self-pity.

That's it. That's precisely it. Simplistic self-pity.

She asks herself, speaking out loud, "Are you tired of it?" Her foot eases on the pedal. Yes, I am tired of it, she answers. Would you have wanted to spend a whole day in the heat, tight in the back seat with Earl and a fussy baby? Heavens no. But the next time someone asks her for breakfast, she might just take that person up on the offer because it is, after all, breakfast, not her life. She has her life—she's a woman in pursuit of a partner. But what if she were a woman in pursuit of adventure? Like now, for instance, the adventure of driving into the mountains in the dark, not sure where she'll stay on the other side? What if she isn't running from anything or running at all? What if she secretly enjoys the freedom of being a single person, acting on a whim to see what happens next?

She slows, opens the window to the rushing wind that embraces her skin, blows her hair, brings with it the refreshing fragrance of pine. And she sees a star. The star—why not—sees her, a driver working her way through the mountains to the sea. All the while, like a whisper in the back of her mind, the radio aches on and on. She listens longingly for a few minutes more, and then, in a surprise move, her hand reaches out, pushes the button. The antenna recedes. She closes the window. Her tears dry. She's all right; there's nothing terrible or sad up ahead. Her headlights know the road.

Galaxy Updraft

Then, due to faulty neurons, inept parenting, and a psychiatric condition that requires consistent management, it starts again: Roz is lost between the kitchen and the bedroom, afraid to move or duck out of sight because dogs the size of pit bulls whine and snarl in the shadows, and anything can happen next—shrapnel might fall from the sky. The dogs have wide, slavering jaws, strong, able teeth. They are dirt brown with yellow footpads and claws like old ivory. They do not care much for people. You can cloy up to them and perhaps curry their favour, curry them, curry up, eat curry.

"Don't go to crazy town, my girl," Roz says out loud. She

makes a fist, knocks herself in the jaw, blinks, and shakes her head. Listens as the dogs scuttle away, back to their invisible hiding places. She looks at her fist. In it she's crumpled a page from a newspaper. The news is bad.

She makes it to the bedroom where the newspapers she collects are carefully stacked against the walls. The stacks are ramparts, surrounding and protecting her mattress on the floor in the middle of the room. In a cardboard box at the foot of her bed she stores her favourite news articles, and among these articles is the years-long story of Margaret Drummond and her little grandson, Brian. Once Cousin Duke asked Roz, "What the hell makes you so fanatic about an old woman and some kid?" Duke is ten years her senior, her only relative, forty-six and divorced. Certain mysteries in life are not fathomable, and the mind, the human mind, is one of them, Roz replied, speaking only to herself. What she might have said out loud to Duke was, "The human mind is a swamp o' misery," making a play on words and imitating his accent. Did Duke appreciate her humour? She can't remember; sometimes he is as volatile as a wind off the ocean, letting kites soar, then suddenly letting them down, leaving them up-ended in the sand.

The latest article, a real shocker, announces that Margaret Drummond is dead. A weekly cleaning woman found the sixty-nine-year-old dead in bed in her little house in Covina. Roz knows the house because she's driven past it. When she had a driver's licence she drove out to Covina and cruised by the house to memorize it. She had wanted to see where Margaret Drummond's grandchild, Brian, was living.

Roz steps over a section of the neat pile of papers, a section slightly lower than the rest, and down into the nestled safety of her bed, onto rumpled sheets and blankets. Then she hears herself whimpering as she reads the article again. Brian is now eleven years old. He was not found in the house when his grandmother was discovered dead, so where is he? His being missing is so distressing. Margaret Drummond may have died of natural causes, but did she? And if she did, was Brian there to watch her die? After all he's been through. The newspaper article seems deliberately vague, as though people shouldn't know the facts just yet. They don't want Roz to know. Why would they conceal the facts from her?

Roz has been following the case of Brian Drummond for three years. His story includes a cruel and neglectful grandmother (Margaret Drummond); a dead father (slammed his plane into the mountain outside of Las Vegas); and a mother no one mentions or knows. According to the news report about Brian's father, "Alcohol may have been involved" in the plane crash. Roz loves that part. Alcohol is a sinner's vice, and Brian Drummond's father, a gambler, was no doubt a libertine. "Of course alcohol was involved!" she shouts.

"Oops, Roz. Oops, Roz." Her hand rushes to her mouth. "Sh, quiet, quiet as a mouse." She listens. The apartment is keeping the peace so far. The building is sweating in the heat;

she can hear the vibrating rumble of a fan in the old man's room upstairs. She has to maintain verbal discipline because of him. If he complains again about a shopping cart racketing down the stairs, full of items she considers useful as well as the newspapers, she will be turfed out to live on the street. She has been warned, first by the landlord and then by a woman from Social Services. That time was an accident, she'd worn the wrong shoes, they tripped her up and she lost her grip. And she was in a hurry. The voices talking about "sinful evillers" and buried babies had quickened, working up to a rampage. That was why she had to rush home.

She breathes and waits. Breathing and waiting is a trick she has learned in order to slow herself down. Out on the street a car door slams, people pound by, a radio plays loud music. She can barely hear the ocean. The reliable white noise of freeway traffic prevails.

She reads the second article, the most exciting and puzzling part of the story. The grandmother (Margaret Drummond) didn't know she had a grandson, yet she was the boy's only relative. Something bizarre must have gone wrong in that family. Roz speculates that the key can be found in the fact that Margaret Drummond, a reading specialist, announced to the world that her son was dyslexic. She was quoted as saying: "My son is dyslexic. I haven't seen him for years." What does being dyslexic have to do with anything?

Roz had cried out when she first read it. Some mothers were

genuinely ungrateful and abandoned their children due to minor problems. And then to be given the gift of a little boy you did not know existed, a little boy related to you by blood—should you not be filled with joy and thank the Lord? Apparently Margaret Drummond was not filled with joy. The eight-year-old had been living with her for one week when he ran away. Of course he was found by the police and brought back.

In the next article, Margaret Drummond is quoted as saying that "the boy" cried a lot. Calling her grandson "the boy" indicates an obvious emotional chasm between them. Roz's own grandmother had lost interest in her too, when she couldn't settle down at school. She was cute and smart one minute, a pariah the next. Margaret Drummond said about her grandchild, "He lacks socialization."

Lacks socialization. Roz dog-paddles her fingers through the articles in the box and finds the only photo of Brian she has. It's blurry, taken when he was first discovered alone in an apartment in Las Vegas. The boy looks like her—hard to pin down, moving fast.

She clambers over the barrier, stands up, and turns in circles. Margaret Drummond is dead. The boy is missing. The reporter wrote that the boy, Brian, has been diagnosed with ADHD. "Of course he's diagnosed!" Roz shouts. "We've all been diagnosed!" In Roz's experience, an ADHD diagnosis is only the cover-up for other, more implicative diagnoses that they are keeping to themselves until further testing.

The man upstairs *rap-rap-raps* the floor with his cane and she shouts back, "Shut up yourself!" Then she tones it down.

Brian is missing. She has to do something. A boy without a mother, as she herself is without a mother, a boy without a father or a grandmother, as she herself is without a father or a grandmother, needs someone to look for him and find him, someone who cares. Two policemen took Roz's driver's licence away on a bad day. But she still has the car.

From the shopping cart in the living room, she takes pairs of shoes and lines them up on the floor. "Are you the ones?" She points to and queries each pair. "You?" Some respond. Some are silent. This behaviour is common; some shoe owners are dead, and their stories are lost. Some have simply moved on. Some shoes are tattletales. Some comedians. Some are boisterous and proclaim outlandishly good times. Some are mousy and want people to feel sorry for them. People feeling sorry for Roz is preferable to them feeling afraid of her. Pity is useful. When people pity you, they feel superior.

She chooses a pair of leather sandals with curled straps. She feels sorry for them. She walks to the front door, turns the handle. The door opens onto a corridor that feels like it belongs to an old ship. "No, no," she says and steps back inside. The problem is the shoes. They're too flimsy and they've not reminded her to bring the car keys. She's distressed by the decision, if it was her decision, to wear such scatter-brained shoes.

She chooses again. A pair of Clarks, black and scuffed on the sides as though the owner's feet rubbed each other. The shoes were made for someone older than Roz, but as she walks back and forth, back and forth between the living room and kitchen, the shoes give her confidence and strength. "Yes."

She walks the shoes into the bedroom and picks up the article and a map of Redondo Beach, where she lives, and a map of Covina, where Margaret Drummond's house is. On the newspaper page an ad jumps to attention: The Electronic Circus. *Bring your kids! Demonstration today!* The game is in a mall in the vicinity of Margaret Drummond's house. A boy whose life is a circus would go there, drawn to a truth that a virtual reality game might reveal to him. Now she understands exactly where she must go. To the mall. Her heart sinks. She and the shoes both know she will need a break after the terrors of the crowds and brassy music they have in that place. She phones Duke and asks if she can stop by. He says, "Don't expect much, the usual drill. I might not be here, but, hey, bring a lobster." Because she lives five blocks from the ocean, Duke thinks that lobsters are as common as cockroaches.

Anybody can stand and watch the players through the glass storefront of the Electronic Circus. "They look pretty dumb," a teenaged boy says. He has a nose ring and orange hair. Roz thought Kool-Aid hair was a thing of the past, but if snarling dirt dogs appear in her consciousness and then escape through her eyes into the real world, then time might be shearing a little, caught in a galaxy updraft. "If you're not fast, a pterodactyl swoops down and grabs you up and drops you. It's like you fall, like, from a plane." The helmeted players stoop, bob, and weave.

Roz feels she should say something to the orange-haired kid. "I'm afraid of heights."

"Oh, you gotta do it."

A woman wearing gold loopy earrings, chewing bubble gum, catches Roz's eye. "He's chicken," she says of the little brown-haired boy beside her. *Pop.* The boy murmurs something and steps behind the woman. "Don't be silly." *Pop.* "You can do it."

"Too bad the game is about shooting people," Roz says.

"Yeah, but it's great." *Pop.*

With this kind of mother loose in a mall, no wonder America is going to hell in a handbasket, a term Margaret Drummond would have used. For all her faults, Margaret Drummond would not have been caught dead chewing gum in public.

Roz looks more carefully at the brown-haired, elusive-eyed boy. An idea occurs to her. Could he be Brian? Could he be Brian who was kidnapped, perhaps by the woman he is with, who would be a terrible mother? The boy has dark eyes and an implacability that Roz recognizes. She turns to him. "Wanna play?"

The woman who's pretending to be his mother pokes his arm. "Go on."

Mostly Roz feels ridiculous in the sweaty helmet, shooting at figures she can't tell apart on a three-tiered screen. The attendant may have forgotten to mention the colour of her character. She might spend the entire game shooting at herself.

The attendant helps her get out of the gear. Because Roz wants to be a good sport, she asks, "Who won?" Half the time she closed her eyes and fired blind, the *rat-tat-tat* of gunshots drilling into her skull.

"He creamed you."

Everyone is gone. The gum-chewing woman. The kid with the orange hair. Brian. New people look in at her through the shiny window, and meaner kids point fingers at her. She remembers those days in the hospital and feels sick to her stomach. She barely makes it to the parking lot, where she throws up. Dirt-coloured dogs circle.

She drives around and around familiar blocks, unable to find Duke's house. Getting lost means she either took too many pills or forgot entirely. Sometimes the meds make her fuzzy; sometimes they make her clear as light from the sun itself. "Dumb fuck," she suddenly utters and instantly regrets the words. The black shoes would not want her to use that language.

Duke's house is white stucco with green window trim. She parks in front, relieved, and breathes deeply. She sees barbecue smoke idling up through the pepper tree in his backyard. She walks across the lawn and through the green latched gate that Duke had to show her how to open and close.

The gate leads to the yard, where on this hot day Duke is likely having himself a cookout with a few cans of cold beer. She is so relieved to see him hunkered in his favourite chair near the grill that tears swell and spill. She wipes her face. Duke does not like crybabies. Roz knows this about Duke and so do his two teenaged daughters, who live with their mother. Duke was in the military and hence does not suffer cowards or the weak-minded.

She sits at the picnic table. Duke stabs one of the three steaks on the grill with his barbecue fork and throws it in the fire. Grey smoke fills the air. Roz is amazed.

"Stephanie didn't come at first call," he says.

Roz has a slump-stomach feeling. "I didn't know the girls were here."

"Just Stephanie."

The girls don't like their father, and despite his having parental rights, sometimes they refuse to come to see him, and when they do bother to visit, sometimes they ignore him. There isn't much he can do. He has a record of domestic violence, so he is being watched as Roz is being watched. A Chinet plate holding a steak and baked potato in foil appears in front of her like magic. Roz takes a bite out of the potato, holding it in her hands. She can't help it; potatoes are a trustworthy food, good in times of need and good for an empty stomach. She chews and swallows and takes another bite.

"I drove by Margaret Drummond's house. There was a police car out front. Unmarked. They're probably waiting for her killer to come back."

"Don't talk with your mouth full."

There was a time when Roz needed reteaching about the basics. Now she needs to recall the basics of communication that others appreciate. "Is everything all right?"

"You ought to know, because you know everything about everything."

"No, no." Roz, astounded, places the remains of the potato carefully back on the plate. "Wow, no. I don't know where Brian Drummond is, nobody does."

Duke puts down his knife after cutting up his steak in bite-sized pieces. "I got this terrible headache. You never think. Maybe I just want to be left in peace, maybe I don't want to have to *listen*."

"Thank you for the food." Roz scrambles up from the table, averting her eyes. She takes a deep breath and ambles back through the gate, latching it securely, goes around to the front of the house and opens the heavy front door. She says hello to Stephanie, who's smoking a joint in the bathroom with the fan on. Stephanie nods. Roz would like to talk to Stephanie, but, as the driver of a car, she should not have marijuana smoke clinging to her clothes. She stops at the threshold of Duke's bedroom. A plan has concocted itself without much thought, and here she is, ready to put it into action. She enters with the intent to steal a pair of his shoes—not black, she's never going to wear black shoes again, might as well call the dogs. She takes the polished brown ones. These may be the shoes he wears to church. His feet are nearly the same size as hers; she doesn't need an extra pair of his socks for padding.

Roz shuts the bedroom door behind her, waves at Stephanie, heads down the front walk in her new shoes. It doesn't pay to be unkind to anyone, she thinks as she drives away. Near home, she finds the right dumpster for the failed Clarks.

It's sundown by the time Roz finds a place to park the car, steps carefully through traffic, and reaches the Redondo Beach pier. Duke's shoes, she notices, are savvy about the hazards of traffic. The surf on either side of the pier has a quiet rhythm, as though slowing down after a hard day. Lights flick on in houses along the strand. Brown pelicans flap by in single file.

The man at the end of the pier is a black man with a soft face. His name is Henry. Henry is an expert about shrapnel, how it falls out of the sky like fireworks, like the Fourth of July, then buries pieces of metal, communication devices, into your skin, contraptions that make you suffer when you least expect it. Roz is not sure about the facts of shrapnel camp, but she doesn't mention her doubts to Henry because she doesn't want to hurt his feelings. Crazy town is more her style. Henry wears a greasy sort of cowboy hat, rim rolled up. As she approaches, she sees familiar gear—his rags and extra poles and, tonight, a dead fish in his orange plastic bucket.

She calls, "Hello?" Henry tips his hat and says, "Good evening," formally, as though they've never met. He seems to like a safe distance between himself and other people. She allows him space. "The day started with dogs. Have I ever told you about the dogs?"

His face crinkles. "Everybody know about dogs." She sees him catch the meaning of her words. He takes a closer look at her. "Oh, you mean *them*. Ain't nobody who is ever lived a life don't know about them."

"Are you sure?"

"Dang I am. I may be old but I still knows a thing or two."

"I have trouble with those dogs sometimes," she says. "And the shoes."

He laughs, showing the gap where a tooth is missing. "Troublemakers, those dang shoes. You spend the day in shrapnel camp?"

Roz nods. However anybody wants to define it, today has not been a good day. Her chest muscles relax and loosen as her lungs open up to the air, salty and spicy with an underlying anxiety of fish. "It kind of took me over. I played a game with a boy in disguise at Electronic Circus and then he disappeared. Why did he disappear like that unless he was hiding? The woman who was acting like she was his mother chewed gum. The real Brian doesn't have a mother. Do you think it was the real Brian?"

Henry takes off his hat, fingers it. "I can't rightly say. You always a gal with real stories to tell."

"I kind of am." The compliment makes her feel bashful. Her hair has been hugging her scalp too tightly the whole drive back. She runs both hands up her neck, pulls strands through her fingers. She looks at Henry, who is waiting for something more. "Gunshots were everywhere. I guess exactly like shrapnel camp. You know a lot about that."

"I does." Henry places his hat back on his head, adjusts it. "That shrapnel, it tell you what to do. Some men's minds get stuck there, can't never get out."

A wave gathers itself, crashes to shore. She asks her question again. "Do you think he was the real Brian?"

"No." The fisherman in Henry returns; the transformation is clear to Roz. His expression changes from worry to serene and lights his face. He points down. "What I think is that dang sea lion's going to take all the fish. You see him out there? He have a big ugly face. Kind of cute, but ugly."

The presence of the fish-eating sea lion would certainly explain the fishes' anxiety. She herself has a little anxiety; the floating beast looks like a huge dog with tiny ears. She holds to the railing.

"See? He happy."

Roz opens her eyes. The sea lion's chocolate-brown pelt isn't like the mangy fur of the dirt-coloured dogs. His eyes are like shiny globes. His whiskers are nice. He seems friendly.

"You just hold tight. It be all right in the end."

Henry offers her a fishing pole. He has never offered her

one of his poles before, and she takes it. They watch the sea lion together. A nice moon is heading toward the ocean, soon to shimmer it. The sea lion barks, a bark totally unlike the sharp yap of a shrapnel-camp dog. Maybe because he likes their company, the sea lion exhibits his clown-like tricks—he barks and disappears below the surface, reappears, splashing, and barks again. Roz and Henry lay their poles on the railing side by side. The sea lion flaps his flippers, then seems contented by his performance and settles back, bobbing in the swells.

At Close Range

Maureen steps out of her condo on the way to the pool and sees a bullet on her Astroturf doormat. A .38 Special. She knows guns, and she knows bullets—she's wintered in Tucson long enough—but finding that damn thing, in the light of day, is unnerving. All the time now, even in her area around the Catalina Mountains, black helicopters clatter in the sky while white Border Patrol vehicles snoop around on the ground. On TV news, SWAT teams hunch outside boxy stucco houses where oversized Fisher-Price plastic toys and cars beyond fixing are strewn around the properties. There is a slick, commercial look to 24/7 media coverage of a society coming undone.

She continues to the pool through the parking lot, carrying her towels and makeup in a straw bag with coloured stripes from Chico's, a women's chain store in a mall across from where Congresswoman Giffords was shot. Leaving the pool area is a young mother in a floral bathing suit cover-up, losing her grip on a fussing, squirming toddler about two or two and a half. The mother sets the blond child down on a patch of lawn, sits on her heels so that she's eye to eye with her, and slides her tanned hands up and down the child's bare back. Maureen pauses to watch. The toddler pulls away and pouts: "Me hungry." The mother murmurs, "Yes, you are feeling so sad, and you are the cutest best baby and you will get Goldfish as soon as we get home, all right? Won't that be so nice?" She glances at Maureen. "Can you believe it? I forgot the cheese crackers."

Maureen unlocks the iron gate and closes it behind her. Joanne is already in the whirlpool, the timer ticking. Maureen does the bookkeeping for Joanne, who hates numbers, in return for half rent. After she puts her things down on a table in the shade, Maureen holds the railing and sidesteps into the swirling green. The two women watch foam roll over their knees. The sky is as blue as Joanne's eyeshadow.

"I would have whacked that kid upside the head," Joanne says. "You should have heard the racket in here a few minutes ago."

"Spoiled." Maureen slips on her visor against the glare.

"Mr. Arnie Jay Jones, the man himself, is gone to the rodeo

with those new folks. Party types." Joanne's husband, Arnie, officially the manager of the Sabrina Springs condominium complex, is useless—only good for high-fivin' around the pool, opening beer, and yakking for the entertainment of the snowbirds, mostly retirees from Wisconsin and Michigan. The rodeo means a day of drinking.

"Some sort of trouble is on the way." Maureen tells Joanne about finding the bullet. She flicks a eucalyptus leaf off her arm, looks at the tree hanging over the pool. A bird scratches in the leaves under it.

Joanne lifts her dark glasses to give Maureen a bug-eyed look. "Is that negativity talking?" Joanne has been listening to self-improvement tapes. The doves along the fence railing scatter, their wings chiming. Joanne sets her sunglasses beside the plastic tumbler on the deck. "Don't start again about Lou," Maureen says. "Lou was just a guy."

"You didn't tell Jennifer, did you?" Joanne reaches for the tumbler and fiddles with the straw as she sips. "This is club soda and white grape juice, just so you know." Joanne is cutting down.

Maureen's daughter has married into a big Estonian family, proud of their cultural identity, and lives in Mississauga, Ontario. She has a little girl and a new baby, a boy. Maureen has seen her four-year-old granddaughter only once. During that visit, Jennifer had muttered, "Never again," as Maureen accepted a third glass of wine from Kurt, Jennifer's father-in-law. Maureen pretended not to hear. But it has been "never again" in terms of a relationship between them.

"Why didn't you tell her?"

"She doesn't want to know," Maureen says. "You know that. We're not simpatico."

Joanne glides off the ledge, sinks into the water up to her neck. "You are some tough."

"Yeah, and you won't dunk and ruin that gunk on your face." Maureen plucks a towel and drapes it over her shoulders so she doesn't burn. Something karmic must be at work in the chronic dislocation with her daughter, her only child. The lie to Jennifer about her father wasn't the world's best idea, she supposes, but she couldn't admit (to anyone) that the father of her baby was a Filipino bus boy at the InterContinental Hotel on Bloor Street in Toronto, where Maureen used to go for a drink after work. Jennifer was conceived in an upstairs staff room. When Maureen told him she was pregnant, he didn't come back to the job; she didn't even know his last name. She checked for him so often that the bar staff scuttled away whenever she popped in. Lying to her daughter as a way out of shame seemed sensible at the time, but the status of Jennifer's invented father—a Brit who died a hero in a fire at an English stadium, and went straight to heaven and became an angel—gave Jennifer lifelong ammunition against Maureen, a mere mortal, imperfect, faltering.

Lou is another story. Him dying in her bed was so damn humiliating—the paramedics working on a corpse with a collapsed, sticky penis. As soon as the ambulance took him away, she phoned the Sally Ann to come get the bed. She made the man work too hard at sex; she should have known better, at his age. They looked like what they were: two people over the hill, trying to whoop it up. Lou may have sold cars, but he was worth loving. They'd been dating, going to movies, checking out lounges featuring light jazz. They both appreciated cold vodka martinis. She liked him. She bought Joanne a case of Henkell Trocken minis and asked her to spread it around the complex that Lou had died in his sleep. No one had better make fun of him.

She kicks a foot, watches the water swirl around her ankle. "It's not like Lou and I were serious."

"Yeah, so? He was a good guy." Joanne hefts herself on to the ledge, her cool fleshy shoulder touching Maureen's. She puts her dark glasses back on. "It's been two months since Lou went. You have to get over it. You're getting bitter as one of those blood oranges they've got at Fry's." Maureen sees Joanne shift gears as she says, "What're you supposed to do with those suckers, anyway?"

After they toss around the merits of the oranges—there was a recipe for blood-orange margaritas in the paper— Maureen leaves the pool, showers, oils every inch of her body, folds herself into a Samoan wrap, and slips on the new sandals with the daisies that look bright against her pretty feet and her toenails, polished a pretty fuchsia.

The phone is ringing when she steps into the apartment. It's Jennifer, words falling from her mouth tinny and mangled, probably calling through the Internet. "The baby doesn't look like anybody in the family."

Maureen touches her fingers to her forehead. Years beyond expecting a greeting like Hello, how are you from Jennifer, she's taken aback by her point-blank words. His eyes? The shape of his eyes? Giving herself time, Maureen lifts the cover off the budgie's cage, and coughs into the phone. "Excuse me. What do you mean?" At lunch, the budgie—it belongs to a friend visiting grandchildren—was squawking, and as soon as he sees her, he starts again. She wags a finger in his face and he hops to the side.

"The baby's eyes aren't normal. Can't you hear me? Are you at it already, this early in the day? What time is it where you are?"

Maureen kicks off her sandals. On the counter is a bottle of tequila; she leaves it in plain sight. In Jennifer's eyes, in the uncompromising severity of her gaze from early childhood on, there was vague distrust, an unwillingness to align herself to her mother, a stranger she didn't quite approve of. The smoking and her choice of friends were "too much," Jennifer had written in a long, earnest letter, the eighteen-year-old truth letter, mailed after she left home, taking with her Maureen's best wool coat, Maureen's money in the form of a plane ticket to London, and eighteen years of Maureen's time. Maureen says, "It's two in the afternoon here, around two. I'm fine. Did you get the baby gift?"

"I'm not talking about your gift, thank you. I'm telling you his eyes aren't normal," Jennifer says again.

Anxiety moves in, grabs hold of Maureen's neck and belly; her body begins to rev up as her mind goes blank. "God. Mongoloid?"

Jennifer falls silent. Maureen expects the slam of the receiver, may deserve it for her callous, unthinking comment.

"Not that." Jennifer sounds tired. "Heredity, the doctor says."

"Are you all right?"

In the ensuing silence, Maureen coughs again, her mind veering off in all directions. Should not have screwed around. Should not have created a pale-eyed father. Should not have found a photo of a decent-looking, ordinary white man, framed it and put it on Jennifer's dresser.

The budgie pipes up again; his voice is a jarring screech.

When Jennifer was born, Maureen hadn't recognized a single feature in the little face, although the infant's skin lightened up after a month and the eyes settled on deep hazel. After weeks of sleepless nights dealing with the surprise baby, she couldn't even remember what Jennifer's father had looked like.

Jennifer is saying, "Maureen? Are you listening? Is this why I don't look like my father? Not really? Is that why I couldn't find my family in England? Is there something you haven't told me?"

Jennifer will hate her even more for the lie; she's the odd one out in her chosen family, has no idea who she is, genetically. Jennifer has no heritage—Jennifer just has Maureen. "Yes," Maureen says.

"Well, what is it?"

Maureen hears Jennifer's impatient, angry breathing, sees the image of the serene young mother on the lawn with her adored child, sees the hugging, the holding, the caressing in the woman's soft words. Maureen can't bear feeling like such a failure and a fraud, and can't begin to frame an apology. She pushes the End Call button. The budgie has tossed seed and pine shavings onto the kitchen floor. She throws a new cuttlebone into the cage, covers the cage up again, moves into the living room, and sits on the divan. The ninth-hole flag whips in the wind. Two couples, neat and tidy, wearing similar outfits, laugh and reach for their hats.

Dressed in pressed white jeans and white boots with metal toes, Maureen stands in line at Marksmen firing range to buy bullets, along with a string of guys who would take it personally if you cut them off on the freeway. The bullets she buys are for personal defence, the type that explode in the body when fired at close range. She's there for the noise, the dead-calm thrill of shooting at shapes of human beings inked in black on yellow paper, seeing the holes rip through them. She loads her new .22 calibre Colt Diamondback bought at a gun show. The gun doesn't have much recoil; it's the perfect size for her hand. The man at the firing range tells her she's good enough for a concealed weapons permit. She knows; she has one, against the law.

She reels in the target sheets, lightly folds them, carries them out to her car. Traffic is heavy, as it always is in winter, people slowing down who don't know the streets. She drives back toward the Catalinas, air conditioning on, the radio tuned to light jazz.

The target sheets feel fragile as she unfolds them. It looks like she has six inky dead men piled on her bed, instead of the one sweet man she actually had, Lou. She carries in a chair from the kitchen and finds a roll of Scotch tape. Picking up the first target, she steps barefoot onto the chair. Carefully, one sheet at a time, she tapes them to the bedroom walls.

With a pitcher of margaritas and a salted glass, she sits on her balcony overlooking the golf course. The wind has died; the mountains are hazy from kicked-up dirt. She can't stop the steady crying, but the umbrella hides the condition of her face. Sometimes drinking isn't the comfort it ought to be. Sometimes it's the same as willfully choosing to back into a closet and shut the door. There is no escape in these trapped moments of despair, and so she's given in to alcohol and remembers when it made her fuzzy, talkative, and confident. This was before she became disgusted with herself for being flirty and assured, before she was just simply not young enough to be so humming and witty. Her head throbs; she's forgotten to take her blood pressure pill.

Tipping the last dribbles from the pitcher, watching the viscous drops slide into her glass, Maureen thinks she probably will have to buy a plane ticket, fly to Ontario. Stay two days in a hotel. Invite Jennifer to lunch, order water, coffee, or tea. If Lou were alive on this day, he would tell that girl a thing or two about respect. He would boost Maureen's spirits, toast her for raising a child on her own, and such a feisty one at that. He would declare in his loud, cheerful voice, "Sleazy-kabeazie, what does anybody care?" But of course someone will care. Jennifer is the responsible girl with the slut for a mother. You can't give birth to a stranger's child and expect to get one who likes you, much less one you know how to raise and cherish.

Maureen stumbles over a footstool in the dark, walks hands-on-furniture to the bedroom. Turns on the lamp, takes the gun from the night table, slides it under the bed. Some things are so screwed up you can never get out of them and never get over them. She raises her head, dizzy, and looks. Graphic figures hanging on the walls come into focus, hearts shredded, shot to bits.

Acknowledgments

For early edits and supportive advice, I thank Luanne Armstrong, Sharmaine Gray, Caroline Adderson, Almeda Glenn-Miller, and Caroline Woodward. For advice near the end, thanks go to my friend Anna Warwick Sears and to Debra Barrett, with her keen eye for art. For their kind consideration over the years, I thank Canadian literary magazine editors, especially Rick Maddocks (*Event*) and Kim Jernigan (*The New Quarterly*). Earlier versions of two stories were published in *Event* and *The Antigonish Review*.

For her willingness to jump into the pile and make some sense of it, my gratitude goes to Nancy Gibson, of Edmonton and Kaslo. For taking it from there, I thank Ruth Linka of Brindle & Glass, and Morty Mint of Mint Literary Agency, Nelson, BC.

Thank you, Lynn Sears, for the use of the Ajo house, and friends, neighbours, and participants in writing workshops, who listened to bits and pieces and offered helpful feedback.

And the "without whom" goes to Rhonda Batchelor, the editor who took these stories further.

HOLLEY RUBINSKY is a Canadian fiction writer living in Kaslo, a village in the mountains of British Columbia. She is the author of *At First I Hope for Rescue* (Knopf Canada; Picador in the US), *Rapid Transits and Other Stories* (Polestar), and *Beyond This Point* (McClelland & Stewart). Winner of the $10,000 Journey Prize and a Gold Medal for fiction at the National Magazine Awards, her second book, *At First I Hope for Rescue*, was nominated for the Ethel Wilson Fiction Prize. Holley was the host of The Writers' Show, produced by CJLY, Nelson. Her stories have appeared in a number of anthologies, including *The Penguin Anthology of Stories by Canadian Women*. Please visit holleyrubinsky.com.